The Lucky Elephant Restaurant

The Lucky Elephant Restaurant

A DETECTIVE LANE MYSTERY

Garry Ryan

Library and Archives Canada Cataloguing in Publication
Ryan, Garry, 1953-
The Lucky Elephant Restaurant / by Garry Ryan.

ISBN-13: 978-1-896300-97-9
ISBN-10: 1-896300-97-9

I. Title.
PS8635.Y354L82 2006 C813'.6 C2005-907686-0

Board editor: Michael Penny
Cover and interior design: Ruth Linka
Cover image: Garry Ryan
Author photo: Karma Ryan

Canada Council for the Arts Conseil des Arts du Canada

Canadian Heritage Patrimoine canadien

edmonton arts council

NeWest Press acknowledges the support of the Canada Council for the Arts and the Alberta Foundation for the Arts, and the Edmonton Arts Council for our publishing program. We also acknowledge the financial support of the Government of Canada through the Book Publishing Industry Development Program (BPIDP) for our publishing activities.

NeWest Press
201–8540–109 Street
Edmonton, Alberta T6G 1E6
(780) 432-9427
www.newestpress.com

1 2 3 4 5 09 08 07 06

PRINTED AND BOUND IN CANADA

for my parents

Thursday, October 8

Chapter 1

"YOU EVER LOOK for a missing kid before?" Harper sat up straight as a high-school principal in a grey sports jacket and matching pants. Their black Chevy crested a hill on John Laurie Boulevard. On their right, Nose Hill Park rose two hundred metres to a plateau of prairie where the city people walked their dogs and kept an eye out for coyotes. To the left, and below, houses were hidden behind a grass-covered sound barrier between the roadway and homes. The treetops were a collage of oranges, yellows, and greens. Over Harper's left shoulder, the downtown high-rises were headstones along the Bow River.

On the western horizon, the Rocky Mountains were white-tipped. In a couple of hours, the sun would drop behind them leaving about thirty minutes of twilight.

"Lane, have you ever looked for a missing . . . ?" Harper said.

"Once," Lane said, finally. "This time, the mother says the child has been missing since yesterday afternoon." He shifted his weight. Looking down the long slope of the road, he spotted a green pickup parked on the shoulder. "Better slow down. Wouldn't want to get your picture taken." There was a white Multi-Nova flash after a speeding Honda passed the truck.

"Should've known." Harper braked. His bear-like hands made the steering wheel look tiny.

They passed the truck. Lane caught a glimpse of the officer waving from the driver's seat. Lane lifted his left hand in return. With his right, he adjusted a purple silk tie. A glimpse in the right mirror assured him that the Windsor knot was at the exact centre of his grey collar. His hand moved to brush white lint from black wool slacks.

"What else do you know about this case?" Harper asked.

"Not much. The father is missing as well. Apparently, he moved out of the house nine weeks ago. He's a welder who travels from job to job. Estranged wife says he went on a holiday. She claims he was angry at her for not letting the kids go with him on a camping trip."

Harper accelerated up another hill.

+ + +

Lane shuddered. A flashback shivered up his spine and filled his nose with the stench of decay. He saw a length of fence. The boards were sun-dried grey. White paint peeled from the wood. It curled into flakes and coated back-alley dandelions. A galvanized trash can had its side creased with a dent. Lane leaned over the can. His fingernails picked at a knot atop a green-plastic garbage bag. It opened. There was a matted mess of curly-blond hair. He'd been told the child's eyes were blue but death, and the light shining through green plastic, changed that. They were a colour he'd never seen before, or since. He stuffed his nose into the crook of his elbow. His voice sounded disconnected. "Over here! Oh, Jesus! Over here!"

He stared down at one blue strap of a pair of denim coveralls looped over the child's shoulder. His heels crunched on gravel. He backed away from the horror and stench of a body swollen by summer heat.

Lane had been there when detectives confronted the father. He'd been drinking. He yelled at Candy. She wet her pants. The father kicked her so hard, she flew into the wall. He put the body in a garbage bag and dropped her into the trash.

Lane remembered getting home that night and throwing his clothes in the wash. Then he scrubbed and shampooed his body till the shower ran cold. For weeks afterward, he smelled death on his clothes, in his hair, and on his hands.

+ + +

"You look kind of pale," Harper said.

"Missing kids." Lane took a breath, shivering as drops of sweat trickled down his ribs. He shook his head. For weeks after he'd discovered the body, a good night's sleep was a memory. "Candy, her name was Candy."

"What?"

"Her name was Candy. The name of the child I found in a garbage can. I hate looking for missing kids. What you usually find is what you can never forget." Lane leaned back and studied the grey fabric around the dome light. Many of those sleepless nights were spent watching TV. One was a documentary about WWII in North Africa. A survivor said, "Flies were everywhere. They fed on the dead. When you swatted a fly, it smelled of death."

Harper opened his mouth to speak, glanced at Lane, and decided against it.

Lane swallowed. The sharp, sour taste of bile caught at the back of his throat.

They stopped at the red light at Sarcee Trail.

Lane said, "Don't know very much yet. The missing child's name is Kaylie. Blond. Four years old. Blue eyes. Has a brother who's eighteen months older. Both live with the mother. Her name's Roberta Reddie."

The light turned green. Harper checked right and left before accelerating. "Roberta Reddie. Isn't that the one on the radio?"

"Apparently."

"Call me Bobbie?" Harper asked.

"The one and only," Lane said.

"No leads yet?"

"Nope. All of the neighbours have been interviewed. Nothing. The dad's nowhere to be found," Lane said.

"Next left?" Harper entered the turning lane before leaving the boulevard.

"Yep." Lane felt anxiety snaking its way up his spine and licking at the nape of his neck.

The Reddie home faced west and sat on a corner with an attached garage on its north side. In the front yard, a pink bicycle lay on its back, white handle bars like outstretched palms lying flat on the grass. Its chain was a sleeping snake, curled over the crank and frame. Flies swarmed around the bicycle and its missing rear wheel.

A champagne-coloured Chrysler sparkled in the driveway. The freshly-waxed paint was tinged rose by the evening sun. Lane wondered at the dirt stuck like clotted blood to the fender liner around the rear wheel. SPK 2ME was written in red letters against the white of the license plate. "Speak to me," Lane said.

"What?" Harper shut off the engine and palmed the keys.

"Vanity plate," Lane said.

Harper looked at the back of the Chrysler. "Oh."

Lane studied the house as he stepped out of the car. The front window was big enough to drive a small sedan through. White sheers curved along either side. The wall facing the window was filled with family portraits above a colonial-style couch. A TV screen blinked like a cursor in the bottom right-hand corner of the window.

Harper rapped twice on the front door. It opened. "Ms. Reddie?"

The woman studied them from behind sparkling glass. Her hair was black and shoulder-length. She wore a black long-sleeved cotton blouse buttoned to the throat. Black slacks. Black socks. Black shoes. Her eyelids were outlined with black eye shadow. "Call me Bobbie," she said. Her voice was low, deep. Bobbie put her back to the wall to let them in. Her generous bust forced them to turn sideways while they inched uncomfortably past her.

Lane's nose filled with her herbal perfume. *It could be described using many words*, Lane thought, *and none of them would be subtle.*

"Have you found her, yet?" she asked.

"We've just started," Harper said.

Lane noted the implied accusation in her voice, and the defensiveness in Harper's reply.

"Tea?" Bobbie asked.

Lane said, "No thank-you. We have some questions, though."

A boy sat in a chair across from the television. He did not look their way.

"Of course." Bobbie indicated the kitchen. "Follow me."

Harper followed.

Lane felt as if she had added a tablespoon of guilt to the contents of his rebellious stomach. He swallowed hard. He put his hand under his nose in an attempt to filter out her scent.

The kitchen's white linoleum was spotless, just like the white appliances and cupboards. The air shone with a chemical mix of air freshener, bleach, and Lysol. Lane checked the sink; no dishes, just polished stainless steel.

Bobbie pointed at the upholstered chairs arranged around the oak kitchen table. "Sit."

Harper sat.

Lane stood.

She moved closer to the sink to fill a kettle with water. "Honey?"

Lane's stomach heaved at a childhood memory of eating too much cotton candy at the Stampede. His mouth filled with saliva.

"This is Cole," Bobbie said. "Say hello to the police, son."

"Hello." Cole was staring at the toes of his white socks.

Lane noted the sharp creases in the boy's white T-shirt and khaki pants. Cole's eyes were blue.

"Would you like some ice-cream, Cole?" Bobbie said the words to her son while smiling at Lane.

"I love Jesus more than ice cream," Cole said.

Bobbie patted his hair without touching his scalp. "Okay, honey. Go back and watch some more television, son."

Lane spotted the immaculate white soles of the boy's socks. A bead of sweat crawled along his hairline from forehead to earlobe. "I've . . ." He clamped his hand over his mouth and headed for the front door. He spotted Cole sitting erect in the chair in front of the TV. There was momentary eye contact between the two. The boy's fear was palpable.

Lane spotted the handle on the screen door. He turned the handle, pushed the door open, took two steps down and breathed fresh air. He crossed the lawn and leaned on the cool metal of the Chevy's rear fender. His belly heaved. He slid his feet back. Lunch poured out onto the pavement. It splattered the black-walled tire and wheel rim. After the fourth heave, he felt a hand on his shoulder. A pair of flies began to circle the edge of the puddle.

"What the hell is going on with you?" Harper asked.

"Don't know." Lane shook his head.

On the way back, along the boulevard, Harper had to pull onto the grass while Lane threw up again. They stopped under a sign next to a church. Lane looked up at the sign. *Bobbie's quote for the week* was written across the top. Under that, *I'm going to heaven. Are you coming with me?*

Chapter 2

THREE KILOMETRES EAST of Bobbie's house, Jay Krocker reached into the bag of almonds on the front seat. Popping the nuts one by one into his mouth, he chewed, and tapped out a beat with his left foot. Six speakers pounded a drum solo against the interior of the Lincoln.

The traffic on Crowchild Trail thinned as the sun ducked behind the Rockies. Purples and reds reflected in the Lincoln's rear and side mirrors.

Jay rubbed his right ear and counted four silver studs, like stepping stones, forming a 'J' along the lobe and auricle. He tucked a strand of black hair behind his ear.

A blur passed Jay on the left. The Toyota pickup cut him off. Jay hit the horn and the brakes at the same time. The rear tires locked and squealed.

The Toyota's driver was just visible over the top of the bucket seat. His arm reached out the open rear-window and extended one finger.

Jay's foot punched the accelerator. The Lincoln took a big swig of gasoline.

The Toyota changed lanes again and cut off a white minivan. The van braked and skidded sideways. It straightened out when its driver released the brakes.

Jay closed on the Toyota.

A fist appeared in the truck's rear-window.

Rage focused Jay. His mind was temporarily uncluttered. He swerved into the right lane.

The Toyota cut in front of him.

Jay hit the brakes and made a feint left.

The truck swerved to block him.

The Lincoln roared. Jay passed on the right. He waited until he was sure he passed the Toyota. Then, he cut left and pressed the brake pedal.

For an instant, he thought the Toyota would rear-end the Lincoln. The truck skidded to avoid a collision. It swerved, bounced over the curb, and onto the grass. It leaned up on its left wheels, before rolling onto its side.

Jay glanced in the rear-view mirror. A cloud of dust obscured the accident scene. His heart pounded with adrenaline. He eased into the far lane, accelerating away from Crowchild Trail.

Chapter 3

"WATER GOOD?" HARPER lifted his glass. The tumbler was nearly opaque from scratches and repeated washings. He looked closely, searching for floaters. First, he held the glass up to the window, then swung it the other way to see if anything showed up against the red cedar on the opposite wall. He set the glass back down, shaking his head with disgust.

Lane took a sip of water.

"You're getting some colour back," Harper said.

Lane leaned against the upholstery and waited.

"You got the flu?" Harper looked around to see where the washroom was.

Lane shook his head. "I don't think so."

"What the hell's the matter then?"

Lane took another sip of water, looked at his partner and shrugged. "Flashbacks."

"Oh." Harper remembered the months of mental reruns following his recovery from being shot. Watching his blood drip down four concrete steps while a screaming man aimed a high-powered rifle. Harper flinched as he recalled what it felt like to be waiting for the muzzle flash.

"Ready to order?" The waitress might have been sixteen. She had a gold stud in her left nostril and another in the right eyebrow. Her hair was crimson, except along the part where the black had grown back in.

"Special looks good." Harper nodded in the direction of the menu printed in red on a whiteboard next to the bar.

"It's better than good." She turned to Lane.

He thought the pink T-shirt shouldn't go with the lime-green slacks, but somehow the fashion faux pas worked for her. "Chicken fried rice, please."

"Drinks?" she asked.

"Water's fine," Lane said.

"Bottled water," Harper said.

"Perrier?" She carbonated the word with sarcasm.

"Long as it's in a bottle." Harper's voice was low. His ears turned red.

"Okay." She turned, took four steps, and pushed through a swinging door into the kitchen.

"Proof is in the food. It's great." Lane looked at the three-year-old calendar, chipped green linoleum, and the table next to them. It had three mismatched chrome chairs that looked like they came from a garage sale. "Despite the decor."

Harper asked, "You gonna explain about the flashback?"

Lane stared at his glass. "My first year on the street. I found Candy's body in a garbage bag. She was three." He experienced a return to the overwhelming dread he had felt in Bobbie's kitchen. "It took six months until I was able to sleep through the night. I kept waking up, remembering the smell. I kept seeing the look on Candy's face. I couldn't stop thinking about what life must have been like for her."

"Those mental carousels go round and round. Believe me, it's hard to get off the ride after when those thoughts get stuck in your head," Harper said.

"Giving advice or trying to change the subject?"

"A bit of both. You're pale. Thought maybe you didn't want to go there again."

"One special." The waitress set an oval plate of rice and ginger chicken with salt-and-pepper vegetables under Harper's nose. "Chicken fried rice." She pushed the second plate over to Lane. The heat breathed a cloud of condensation up the side of his water glass.

"That was quick," Harper said to the waitress.

"And delicious." She slid a bottle of Perrier in front of Harper.

The detectives ripped open paper-wrapped chopsticks.

Harper said nothing for a full five minutes while demolishing the special. "Man, this is the best Chinese food I've ever tasted."

Lane swallowed a mouthful of fried rice. More than three-quarters remained. "My kind of place."

Harper cocked his head to the right to study Lane.

"Decor is nothing at all like the food," Lane said.

"Trying to teach me another lesson?" Harper asked.

"What would that be?"

"Look past appearances." Harper pointed a pair of chopsticks at his partner.

"Wasn't really thinking about that." To himself, Lane thought, *Now that you mention it.*

"So, what's our next move?"

"Find out more about the father," Lane said.

"And?"

"Bobbie." Lane looked thoughtful.

"What about her?" Harper asked.

"We need to talk with people who know more about her."

A cellphone rang. They both reached inside their jackets.

Lane flipped his open. "Hello."

"It's me," Arthur said.

"Something the matter?" Lane asked. Arthur almost never called him at work. There was anxiety in his voice.

"Are you going to be very long?"

"Could be there in a half-hour," Lane said.

"Good," Arthur said.

"What's going on?"

Arthur said, "It's not the kind of thing to be explained over the phone. I'm fine. Riley's fine. A surprise arrived on our doorstep."

"On my way." Lane closed the phone. He looked at Harper.

"Don't look at me. The baby started kicking. I'm heading home to see Erinn."

+ + +

The odour tweaked Lane's nose when he walked around the side of their house. Arthur had the flowerbeds ready for winter. The perennials, mostly wildflowers, were trimmed back. The rest were replaced with freshly-turned earth. This new odour wasn't the manure Arthur mixed with the soil. This was sweat. Old sweat. Athlete sweat.

At the back doorstep, Riley had his nose jammed into a blue-and-white equipment bag. The shaft of a goalie stick poked out one end. Riley was deep in the nose zone. He could get so hooked on a scent that he became oblivious to all else. In the summer, it had earned him a snoot full of porcupine quills.

Riley looked at Lane, drooled, and barked once. Loping over, he wagged his tail and got a scratch under the chin from Lane. Then he turned, ran, and stuck his nose back inside the bag. Lane pulled the bag onto the grass and Riley followed. The screen door was open part way. Lane heard an unfamiliar voice.

"Dad's a fag! Dumped my mom. She can't have any more kids. He says he's a leader in the community. If she can't have any more kids, he has the right to marry somebody else. Two days ago, he told her he wanted a divorce. Then he put her stuff in the garage and changed the locks. When I called him a hypocrite, he kicked me out too. Mom thinks he's got some woman pregnant and wants to marry her," the young male voice said.

"How's your mother?" Arthur asked.

"Fine. Stayin' with a friend. Had to get out of that small town. Everyone is talkin' about her, blamin' her 'cause my Dad's tellin' everybody she drove him to it. It felt good to get out of there."

Lane thought, *I must look ridiculous eavesdropping*

at my own backdoor. He opened the door and said, "Hello."

There was the sound of a chair being pushed back.

Lane put one shoe on the second step, bent to untie the lace, then shifted feet.

Arthur stood at the top of the steps, in a blue T-shirt and black sweatpants. The crotch hung halfway to his knees. Light reflected off his thinning hair and round, Mediterranean face. "Matt is here," Arthur said.

Lane heard a mixture of shock and hope in Arthur's voice. Lane thought, *Matt who?*

Reading the question on Lane's face, Arthur said, "My sister's son."

All Lane had just heard fell into context. He stepped into the kitchen, studying the boy sitting at the table eating a cowboy-sized mouthful of sandwich. Matt looked to be fifteen with blond hair in desperate need of a brush. Lane spotted a green garbage bag in the corner. *It's full of Matt's clothes*, Lane thought.

In order to get a better look at Lane, Matt hooked his arm across the back of the chair. His face was round like his uncle's. The skin around his eyes was puffy from crying. There was a pimple sprouting at the end of his nose.

Tentatively, Lane reached out with his right hand. Matt took it in a quick, firm, herky-jerky grip before releasing. The boy smelled like the country. Lane slipped off his sports jacket. The black butt of his handgun poked out from its holster.

Matt's eyes widened as he noticed the Glock.

"Ever seen one of these?" Lane asked.

Matt shook his head, "Nope."

Lane turned so Matt could get a better look at the Glock.

Matt leaned closer.

Arthur said, "No guns in this house! I don't ever want it in the house again."

After Matt went to bed, Arthur and Lane sat in the living room. Arthur had his feet up on the coffee table. His fingers were wrapped around a cup of tea. The cup rested under his breasts atop the curve of his belly. He sat at one end of their L-shaped couch with Lane at the other.

Lane said, "I was only showing the gun to Matt. I've never met the kid before, and I could see the interest in his eyes."

"The boy's fifteen, his parents just split up, and I don't want that damned thing in the house! Is that too much to ask?"

"Where's your sister?" Lane asked.

"She's staying in town. Don't try to change the subject. That fucking gun can't stay here anymore!"

"Why?" Lane asked.

"Because when I was fifteen I put a goddamned gun in my mouth. If it hadn't been for Martha, I would have pulled the trigger. Lock it up somewhere safe. I won't be able to sleep with the damned thing around. Oh, and that was on the doorstep when I got back from picking up Matt at the bus station."

"What are you talking about?" Lane asked.

Arthur pointed at the newsletter under the coffee table. "I saw Mrs. Smallway bring it over." Arthur got up and left.

Lane picked up the folded paper. As he read, he noticed that someone had taken the trouble to underline some of the editorial page from *The Daughters of Alberta Newsletter*.

SWATSKY CASE MAY REVEAL DISTURBING BIAS IN CALGARY POLICE FORCE

Important questions surrounding the death of Robert Swatsky remain unanswered.

Amid charges of fraud, missing money (estimated at $13 million), the disappearance of the victim's ex-wife, and accusations aimed at the ex-mayor, the truth behind Robert Swatsky's violent death has yet to be revealed.

It appears that a powerful group within the Calgary police force prefers to keep it that way. A powerful group with a flagrant disregard for family values.

The main question remains unanswered. Who killed Robert Swatsky? The coroner's report was inconclusive. The prime suspects, Ernesto Rapozo and Leona Rankin, died under suspicious circumstances, and within minutes of one another. They have become convenient suspects.

It would have been impossible for the sixty-eight-year-old Rankin (who suffered from emphysema) to kill Swatsky. The seventy-year-old Rapozo would have had difficulty disposing of Swatsky's three-hundred pound body.

Rapozo and Rankin are unlikely criminals. Apparently, the police have closed this case. Internal sources confirm that the reasons for this lie at the feet of the senior police detective in charge of the case. A detective who may have his own reasons for hiding the truth.

Sunday, October 11

Chapter 4

JAY DROPPED THE wet mop into the bucket of soapy water. White froth heaved from one side to the next. The castered wheels rocked back and forth. His nose filled with the raspberry scent of chemical soap. On one side of the aisle were rows of bras in flat, perfectly-proportioned cardboard packages sporting vertical smiles. On the other, dresses and pantsuits hung on mannequins. It was three hours after store closing, and his shift would soon be over.

He reached for the tape player on his hip and flipped the cassette over. While resolving to buy new technology, he started side two of today's psychology lecture. *Hope this gets my mind off what happened to the guy in the Toyota*, he thought. Jay said out loud, "Why do I always have to run away?"

Dr. Peters' voice was a familiar blend of gravel and a long-time acquaintance with single-malt scotch. "According to the dictionary, a sociopath exhibits a lack of social or moral responsibility while a psychopath is characterized as amoral and/or antisocial. The reality, as is often the case, is quite different from the dictionary definition." Jay wrung the water out of the mop. He began a long series of wet lazy figure-eights braided into a shiny, liquid coating over the linoleum. Dr. Peters said, "Individuals with the aforementioned pathologies often appear to be well-adjusted, even successful."

A tricycle swept past on Jay's left. Startled, he slipped. His legs and arms windmilled to keep him from falling.

The tricycle spun on the wet floor. Tony hunched over the handlebars with knees and elbows bent at odd angles. His black hair spun out with the centrifugal force. The trike stopped. Tony's hair fell around his eyes. He eased off the child's toy till he stood about one-hundred-and-eighty centimetres. "Hey Jay."

"The key to identifying the psychopath—" Dr. Peters was interrupted when Jay shut the tape off.

"Listening to music?" Tony asked.

Jay hooked the headphones around his neck.

"I got finished early and decided to take a spin. Sorry about the floor." He picked up the trike by one handlebar and tiptoed off the wet to stand beside Jay.

"Hey!" Walter said with his best-boss voice. "You FOB prick! What are you doin' down here? You're supposed to be upstairs!"

Jay and Tony turned to face Walter. His hair was blond and combed over to hide an ever-expanding bald spot. "I could fire you right now."

Jay leaned out. He swept the mop over the marred surface till it shone once again. "For what?"

"For being down here when he's supposed to be working upstairs." Walter jammed his fists onto his hips.

"You should be rewarding him for finishing ahead of time. Besides, what exactly does FOB stand for? You wouldn't be saying *fresh off the boat*, because you wouldn't make a racist remark like that! I mean, our employer must have some policy against discrimination in the workplace," Jay said.

Walter's eyes narrowed. He pointed a finger first at Tony, then at Jay. "I'm gonna keep a close eye on you two." He turned, unhitched the keys attached to his belt and walked away.

"Sorry man. Didn't know he was hangin' around," Tony said.

"It's okay." Jay dipped the mop in the bucket.

"What kind of music you listenin' to?"

"It's a lecture on psychopathy." He tapped the tape player.

"Is there a case study about Walter?" Tony asked.

"Haven't got into obsessive-compulsive disorders yet."

Tony picked up the trike. "Thanks for sticking up for me. You've been doing that since we were in high school."

"What are friends for?"

+ + +

Tony sat in the passenger seat. "You've gotta meet my Uncle Tran."

They drove north on Macleod Trail. "Why the big rush?" Jay was a bit taken aback by Tony's insistence. And afraid. Afraid of what Tony might discover.

"I phoned him. Told him how you stuck up for me and stood up to Walter. Uncle Tran said, 'It's time to bring that Jay to see me'. You don't understand what a big deal this is."

Jay looked right at St. Mary's Cemetery then to the Chinese Cemetery on the left. He thought about where he was going to sleep tonight. He almost turned the radio on to find out if the Toyota driver had been hurt and if the police were looking for him. *No, leave the damn thing off*, Jay thought.

"It's real close to where you drop me off in Chinatown. The food's free. So is the parking," Tony said.

"Okay."

Ten minutes later, they stood outside The Lucky Elephant Restaurant. The neon sign was off and a closed sign was in the window. The lights were still on inside. Tony tapped on the door. A man stood. Jay almost missed him at first. He was in the corner, in shadow. His hair was white. He stood within a couple of centimetres of five feet. He wore a blue shirt, a pair of black Levi's, and white running shoes. The man smiled widely and opened the door. He said, "Please, come in." He had a gentle, singsong accent that Tony sometimes imitated.

"My name is Lam Tran. Uncle Tran." He gently shook Jay's hand and indicated they should sit at the back of the restaurant. Tony and Jay sat on either side of Uncle Tran.

The face of the cook appeared in the window of the kitchen's swinging door.

Jay noticed Tony's unnatural reticence.

"You like satay soup?" Uncle Tran made conversation sound like music. "It's the best in the city."

Jay hesitated, going over the words in his mind, making sure he understood the accented English. "Sure."

Tran lifted three fingers. The cook nodded and disappeared.

"Tea?" Uncle Tran asked. His black eyes never left Jay.

"Please." Jay glanced at Tony who looked elsewhere as if to indicate that Jay was on his own. Tran poured tea into three small cups. He met Jay's eyes with steady appraisal. On Tran's cheek, a finger-wide scar ran along the bone beneath his right eye. Jay asked, "What happened?"

"You have to remember, Uncle," Tony said, "Jay has ADD. It's called attention deficit disorder. He means no disrespect. He just blurts out whatever is on his mind."

Tran set the teapot down and ran his index finger along the scar. "My village was caught in the middle of a battle between the Viet Cong and the Americans. I was a very lucky child. It was an American bullet."

"How do you know it was an American?" Jay regretted his words as they left his mouth.

"The soldier was very close. I looked into his eyes when he fired his M-16."

Jay sipped his tea to stop himself from asking more questions. The herbal scent was pleasantly unfamiliar. He felt irretrievably out-of-place.

Tran said, "My nephew says you have been very helpful. A true friend. You have known each other since high school. He speaks often of you and your good character. There have been many times he has been grateful for your support. Tony has been telling me about you for two years."

Jay shrugged. He was embarrassed and curious. The kitchen door swung open. The cook backed out with a tray holding three steaming bowls of soup and a plate piled high with bean shoots and quartered limes. Beginning at Uncle Tran, he slid the bowls onto the table. The cook left the tray on the table, nodded at Tran, and went out the front door, carefully locking it behind him.

Uncle Tran used chopsticks to grip a slice of tomato. Delicately, he lifted the red circle to his lips and nibbled.

Tony used a spoon to slurp the broth.

Halfway through the meal, the spicy heat of the satay soup radiated to Jay's extremities.

Uncle Tran used a napkin to wipe sweat from his forehead. "You've chosen your friend wisely, nephew."

"Thank you, Uncle," Tony said.

Jay felt warmth and dread bubbling up from the risks of acceptance. *After all,* he thought, *I don't come from a healthy gene pool.* He looked for an exit.

Tony laughed. "You should have seen Walter's face when Jay asked what FOB meant. Uncle, it was a priceless moment."

Jay laughed and listened as one story lead to another. One, in particular, stuck with him.

Tony badgered his uncle to explain how he'd come to Canada.

Tran surrendered gracefully. "I was in Saigon. The Americans were leaving. Some of us had visas for Canada, but we could not get official permission to leave Vietnam. The embassies were closed. It was chaos." Tran hesitated.

Jay had the distinct impression Tran was about to stop, because he'd said too much.

"Please, Uncle," Tony said.

"There was so much confusion. I went to the airport. Some of the embassy staff were loading their limousines onto transport aircraft. So many people trying to leave, and they took the cars!"

Jay noticed the tears in Uncle Tran's eyes.

"I walked up to the aircraft. Near one of the cars was a box wrapped in black fabric. I picked it up, walked onto the aircraft, and hid. We landed at night. I carried the box off the plane."

"Tell him what was in the box!" Tony said.

"A jade elephant." Tran smiled as he stared into the past.

"It's over there." Tony pointed to a shelf behind the bar. The elephant stood with its curled trunk touching the top of its head. It looked like it was smiling.

Monday, October 12

Chapter 5

HARPER PRESSED "PLAY."

Bobbie's radio voice was smooth as butter on a fresh-from-the-oven muffin. "Vivaldi. *Four Seasons.* One of my favorites." A three second pause. "As some of you already know, my daughter has been abducted. This morning's show will be devoted to the topic of missing children. I'm Bobbie. Speak to me."

Harper hit "Stop." The scent of coffee filled the air between them. Lane leaned forward to listen more carefully to the voice. They were in a room with space for a table, four chairs, and two people. Harper pressed "Play" again.

"We're back. This morning's topic is missing children. My daughter disappeared a few days ago. We had her birthday party recently. My ex-husband was there. He demanded he be allowed to take the children on a camping holiday. I declined. Now, my daughter is gone. The police have yet to find my ex-husband or my Kaylie."

Harper hit "Pause." "Her ratings have been increasing since she started up a little over a year ago. She sounds sincere." He sipped coffee.

"Think so?" Lane stared at the white wall.

"You don't?"

"No."

"You may be the only person in the city who thinks

that way. She's very popular." Harper released the pause button.

Bobbie said, "This is a direct appeal to my ex-husband. Charles! Bring our daughter back. Cole misses her desperately. Bring our child home." A three second pause. "I know I'm not the only woman who has gone through this. I want to hear from others like me. What happens to mothers who go through what I'm going through? How do I cope?"

Lane stabbed the "Pause" button. "What else do we know about her?"

"You want me to find out, right?" Harper asked.

"Yes," Lane said.

"What about the father?"

"That's my job." Lane leaned back.

"What do you need to know about Bobbie?"

"Her past. People who've known her for a long time," Lane said.

"Why, in particular?" Harper opened his laptop. It chimed after he pressed the power button.

"Just curious," Lane said.

Harper looked over the laptop at his partner.

Lane asked, "How come we never see her face anywhere? The promos show her hands or the back of her head. Never a face. How come? I want to hear from the people who know her best."

"Maybe a little mystery helps sell the show." Harper tapped they keyboard.

"Maybe. Maybe not," Lane said.

"Why aren't we looking for the father?"

"Every cop in Canada and the US is looking for him. His camper is missing. I don't think we'll find them in the city, so we have to rely on someone else," Lane said.

"You're assuming they'll be found together."

"Yes," Lane said.

"So, why am I looking into Bobbie's past?" Harper asked.

"I've lost objectivity when it comes to Ms. Reddie. We've got to have as much information as possible about her when dad and daughter are found."

"What happens if they're never found?"

"We have to work on the assumption that they will be," Lane said.

Harper shook his head. "I still think we should check into the father's background."

"That's my job," Lane said before leaving the room.

Tuesday, October 13

Chapter 6

SUNRISE TAKES TOO *long this time of year,* Lane thought. *I've become used to summer days when the sun is up by five-thirty and doesn't set till ten o'clock.*

Now, at eight o'clock, the sun was warming the kitchen. He stood, stretched, and soaked up the rays. The coffee maker spluttered its last drops over the freshly-ground Arabica beans. He rubbed at the ache in his left hip, leftover from sleeping on the couch.

Riley's toenails pattered along the floor. The retriever grazed Lane's leg to say good morning, then moved to the dining room where he settled down for a nap under the table.

Lane heard the toilet flush. The water rushed through the pipes under the kitchen floor. *I wonder if sleep has softened Arthur's mood,* Lane thought. He poured a coffee for himself and another for Arthur—a peace offering. Arthur's slippers scuffed down the hall and into the kitchen.

Lane thought, *If he's slept more than an hour, it doesn't show in his eyes.* They were red-rimmed with dark half-circles underneath. A tuft of hair stuck out at right angles above his left ear. Arthur reached for the cup of coffee, then added sugar and milk. A spoon clinked against the cup. He took a sip, closed his eyes, sighed, took a longer sip, then said, "Thanks."

They sat in silence through a cup and one-half.

Arthur said, "I've got to get Matt into school and hockey."

Lane was on the edge of saying, "Shouldn't we talk about this?" Instead, he said, "How's Martha doing?"

Arthur looked out the window, closed his eyes and said, "She's in the Tom Baker Cancer Centre."

Lane thought of at least ten questions. Instead, he decided on a sip of coffee.

"It's breast cancer. They're operating this morning. She made me promise not to tell Matt. She says he's lost his home, his friends, and his father. Finding this out about her will be too much for him. She says, 'He's not as tough as he lets on.' I always hoped I'd get a second chance to know my sister. I never imagined it would be like this, but. . . . "

"You're going to have to tell Matt," Lane said.

"I promised."

"He's probably already figured it out. He's a smart kid. Takes after his uncle. Besides, how is she going to explain away the hair loss from the chemo?" Lane asked.

Arthur wiped a sleeve across his eyes.

Lane said, "Matt's father is big on family values. He wouldn't allow Martha to have anything to do with you or me. Last we heard, he was a big wheel in his church. How will he react when he finds out Matt is living with us?"

"How will he find out?" Arthur asked.

The phone rang.

"It's not a matter of how. It's a matter of when. We

have to be prepared for that eventuality." Lane picked up the phone. "Hello?"

Arthur stared at the coffee grounds at the bottom of his cup.

Lane said, "We'll need a map. As usual, you're way ahead of me. See you in a half-hour."

Arthur looked up when he heard the ice-cold tone of Lane's voice. "What's happened?"

Lane held up his hand to get Arthur to wait. "As long as it's cleared with the Mounties." He hung up the phone.

"The girl?" Arthur asked.

"And the father." Lane looked out the window and into the back alley. "A forensic team is on the scene. Initial indications are murder/suicide."

+ + +

By ten o'clock the road west of Calgary was free of commuters. The foothills rose up on the north side of the two-lane highway. On the south, the Bow River gathered breadth as it ran away from the mountains. Oranges, yellows, and reds were falling from the trees. Pastures on either side of the road were still green. More and more pine trees were in evidence as they approached the Rockies. Lane read the map. Harper drove in silence.

"It's the next right," Lane said.

Harper coasted, then braked before turning north onto a paved and frequently-patched road. It was just wide enough for two vehicles. They climbed a hill. Snow crept down the shoulders of the peaks on their left.

Lane paid close attention to the map and directions. They took a series of turns onto progressively narrower gravel roads. He wondered how the Mounties had been able to find the camper. "There." Lane spotted an RCMP cruiser blocking the road.

Harper pulled up to the cruiser. He parked and turned off the engine.

Pine branches brushed Lane's door as he got out. He felt the promise of winter in the breeze coming from the north.

The RCMP officer approached them. A single braid of black hair brushed her gun belt. She asked, "You are?"

"Detectives Lane and Harper," Harper said.

"Been expecting you. The camper's over there." She pointed to a trail turning left off the main road. "Couple of guys on dirt bikes found it."

"Thanks," Lane said. He and Harper followed the trail for about thirty metres. Grass grew knee-high between parallel tracks of compacted earth. Above them, the trees on either side of the trail reached out to touch limbs. A squirrel chattered a warning.

They found the forensic van parked in front of a blue truck with a white camper perched on its back. Investigators looked like they were part of a Michelin Man convention, in their crime scene bunny suits and masks. One stood next to the open door of the truck. Charles' corpse sat in the front seat. The investigator's camera flashed, freezing the scene in Lane's mind.

Charles' eyes and mouth were open. His head was cocked to one side, posed in that position. Duct tape sealed the partly-open window on the passenger side. A length of flexible black plastic pipe led from the window. It wound around the side of the truck to the exhaust.

The photographer said, "Stay about five metres out when you walk around the campsite. The father's here," he nodded at the body, "and the daughter's in the back."

Harper and Lane moved around the front of the pickup. Lane noted that the windshield was starred on the passenger side. Eight cracks traveled away in different directions from the centre of the star. The detectives stayed clear of the truck and moved to the back where a single lawn chair sat facing a campfire ringed with stones. Between the fire and the camper, a picnic table sat under a blue tarp attached to the back of the camper. The stench of decomposition blended with the scent of leaves rotting on the ground. Lane concentrated on the scene and not the emotions evoked by memories of death and rot.

He saw that a recent rain had erased most of the footprints. The only fresh tracks had been made by the tires of a motorcycle. Today's footprints were indistinct hollows left by the forensic team's overboots. All of them wore fibre masks over their mouths and noses. One walked slowly along the edge of the clearing, studying the ground. Another walked farther out and disappeared behind a ten-metre pine tree.

Lane and Harper stood near the campfire. They

turned to look in the back door of the camper. The smell of death seemed strongest here. There was an investigator inside the camper. Beside her, on the bench, was the body of the child. Blond hair, blue jeans, and sneakers. The soles of her shoes were white and the treads free of dirt. The investigator backed up, nudged one of the child's shoes, and its heel flashed red.

The investigator turned toward them. Her eyes focused on Lane. She nodded. He returned the gesture. She extended the pinkie and thumb on her right hand, and held it to her ear to indicate she would phone him.

Lane nodded.

She turned back to the child.

Lane walked away from the scene and back down the trail to their car. He thought, *This isn't the first time you've seen a dead child. You survived the last one. At least this time, you're not alone.*

Harper followed in silence till they were seated inside the Chev. He started the engine. Both reached to open their windows.

Harper said, "The woman in the camper. What was that all about?"

"It's Lisa. An old friend. We've worked together before. She's going to give me a call later. I'm not sure what it's about." Lane could smell death on his clothing and wondered if it would wash out this time.

+ + +

Five minutes later, in the university parkade, Jay's watch beeped. He pulled his right arm from inside the confines of his Mountain Equipment Co-Op sleeping bag and checked the time.

A car door slammed nearby and an alarm chirped. The rumble of a broken muffler echoed inside the parkade.

Jay stretched so his feet pushed against one door and nudged his head up against the other. He thought, *Man, whoever designed this bench seat knew about comfort.*

His work and class schedules were taped to the back of the front seat. He stuck a finger on the timetable and said, "Psychology 2:00 PM." He thought, *If I get up now, there'll be time for a workout, shower, and lunch.* He lifted his head, took a look around, then began to pull on a pair of sweatpants.

+ + +

"We've got news about your daughter," Lane said. He and Harper stood just inside Bobbie's front door.

Bobbie's face was perfectly made up; black eyeliner and eye shadow, rouge on the cheeks, and glossy-red lipstick. "My daughter? You found her! Where is my Kaylie?"

"We found her and your ex-husband in his camper. It was west of Cochrane and near the mountains," Lane said. Harper stood behind him.

Bobbie stood in the hallway. Her voice rose as she asked, "My daughter is okay?"

"No, she's not," Lane said.

"My baby's dead?" The volume of Bobbie's voice rose even higher.

"That's correct," Lane said.

Bobbie turned away, then turned back to look at Lane. She wrapped her arms around his neck and buried her face against his shoulder. "My baby! My God! My baby!"

Lane looked into the room where Cole stood in the hallway. Tears ran down his cheeks. He cried silently, never taking his eyes away from Lane.

"My baby! My God! My Kaylie!" Bobbie cried.

Lane and Harper had to carry her between them to get her to the couch.

Cole stood at least three metres away, crying and watching Lane. Tears dripped from the boy's cheeks, forming two circles of translucent white on the front of his T-shirt.

Chapter 7

LANE WIPED A towel across his face. He inhaled the scents of soap, shampoo, and death. The light on the phone blinked red, indicating a message was waiting. He pressed the button on the left side and heard Lisa's voice. She had two voices. He'd known both of them for more than a decade. One was a friendly, happy-go-lucky voice she always used around her partner, Loraine. The other was a controlled, police voice she used right now. "I've got preliminary information and some anomalies. Call me at home."

Lane hung up. In the quiet, he heard the washing machine shift into spin cycle. His clothes had gone into the wash before he stepped into the shower. *I'll have to throw them away if the smell doesn't come out*, he thought. He remembered that after leaving Bobbie, he'd removed his jacket. There had been no moisture mixed in with the makeup residue on the shoulder of his jacket. Lane dialed Lisa's number.

She answered after the third ring. "Lane?"

"How are you?" he asked.

"Not one of my better days." She took a breath. "There are some inconsistencies."

"Go on," Lane said.

"There are no fingerprints on the duct tape used to seal the cab of the truck."

"Why would he go to the trouble of leaving no prints, if he was about to commit suicide?" Lane asked.

"Exactly. There are more contradictions. We'll have to wait for the autopsy, but I don't think the father died of carbon monoxide poisoning," Lisa said.

"What about the child?"

"The cause of death will have to wait for the autopsy," Lisa said. "But, I did find a torn piece of plastic in the waistband of her pants. It looks like it came from a garbage bag."

"She was wrapped in it?" Lane had a flashback of finding Candy in the garbage bag.

"It looks like her head and torso were wrapped up. Then the bag was tucked into her waistband."

Lane remembered Kaylie's shoes. "Did you see the soles of her shoes?"

"Too clean for a kid on a camping trip?"

"Yes," Lane said.

"That's about all I have right now. Just thought you'd want to be kept up to speed. You didn't stick around for very long."

"No."

Lisa waited for an explanation that wasn't coming, then said, "Say hello to Arthur for us."

"You bet. And pass on our regards to Loraine." Lane hung up. *This could get really messy*, he thought.

Fifteen minutes later, the phone rang.

"Lane?" There was an anxious excitement in Arthur's voice.

"What's the matter?" Lane asked.

"I'm signing Matt up for hockey."

"Oh. That's nice."

"The team is run by volunteers," Arthur said.

"And?" Lane became anxious with where this conversation was headed.

"They've already got a coach and a manager."

"That's good." Lane was relieved but still uneasy.

"The team needs a referee."

"You've got to be kidding!" Lane said.

"You can skate," Arthur said.

"Figure skate."

"Exactly. They need a person who can skate."

"I don't know the rules," Lane said.

"They have a course."

Lane heard the voices of parents talking over each other. "No way."

"You'll be going to Matt's games anyway. This way you can get some exercise at the same time. Get your mind off work. Besides . . ."

"Besides?"

Arthur said, "I already signed you up. And, they gave us free tickets. We're going to a hockey game tonight."

+ + +

"CKKY, KY Radio, regrets to announce that Bobbie will not be on the air today. She's taking time off due to the death of her daughter. Bobbie sends her appreciation for the kind wishes and prayers of her listeners. We'll be playing *The Best of Bobbie* until she returns."

+ + +

Jay surveyed the kiosks on either side of Mac Hall. The

lineup at The Noodle House was at least fifteen minutes long. Other lineups formed at burger, coffee, and taco shops. *I beat the rush*, he thought, while using chopsticks to maneuver noodles, beef, and mushrooms into his mouth. For five bucks he could eat and watch the people go by.

"Hey cracker, you're pretty good with chopsticks," Tony said. He sat down next to Jay and leaned his back against the table. Tony set his backpack on the floor.

"You're late." Jay slurped an especially long noodle.

"This guy in the front row kept asking questions." Tony used his fingers to grab the last piece of beef from Jay's plate.

"Hey!" Jay tried to stab Tony with the chopsticks.

"Too slow. We still on for Rex's game tonight? I've got the masks," Tony said.

"You ever gonna let that guy off the hook?"

"No. Not after he got my cousin pregnant, and the way he treated Uncle Tran."

"How's your cousin doin'?" Jay wiped his chin with a paper napkin.

"Okay. The baby's getting big. Uncle Tran got them a place. He's helpin' out with school and daycare," Tony said.

"Uncle Tran's restaurant must be doin' well. He got you and your mom a house and helps you with school," Jay said.

Tony laughed, "His money's in elephants."

"What's that supposed to mean?"

"The lucky elephant in the restaurant," Tony said.

"Yeah, I saw it. Uncle Tran said he picked it up in Saigon and carried it onto a plane."

"That's right. And, on the long ride over here he found out the elephant was hollow," Tony said.

"So?" Jay asked.

"The plane landed at night. Uncle Tran slipped away. He disappeared with the elephant."

"What are you sayin'?" Jay asked.

"Uncle Tran lost everything and everyone in Vietnam. He picked up a lucky elephant and started a new life," Tony said.

"How can he be your uncle if he lost everyone?"

Tony appeared to be staring at the spiral staircase leading to The Aboriginal Friendship Centre. "He's not my real uncle. My mom and I are refugees. Just the two of us. My cousin with the baby, she's not my real cousin. She and her mother were in the same situation. Uncle Tran adopted us, and we adopted him. Now, we're a family and help each other out."

"So, how does the elephant fit in?" Jay asked.

"It's Uncle Tran's story to tell." Tony stood up. "Come on. We've got some planning to do."

+ + +

"Want some popcorn?" Arthur asked Matt as they entered Father David Bower Arena.

"And a hot dog?" Matt wore a new blue T-shirt, red jacket, and black running shoes.

Lane watched the boy closely. There was a slight hitch in the way he walked. *He hardly talks when he walks because he's so busy concentrating on not falling,* Lane thought. *Arthur has been waiting a long time to spoil a nephew or niece. I wonder what will change between them when Matt finds out his mother has cancer?* Lane watched Arthur, and his nephew, and felt a mixture of joy and foreboding.

"You want something?" Arthur asked.

"No, thanks," Lane stepped close to a cinder-brick wall. The arena brought back memories of early mornings and figure skating. Jibes from boisterous hockey players jogged his memory. One particularly vicious experience surfaced. A dark-haired, teenaged hockey player once used the blade of his stick to jab a twelve-year-old Lane just below the ribs. Lane remembered gasping for air and dropping to his knees. The player then said, "Just another fag in tights."

Lane looked up. He saw tonight's fans arriving in dribs and drabs. They bought food and drinks at the concession before wandering through the heavy metal doors to the stands.

By the time Arthur found a place to sit near centre-ice, Matt had finished the hot dog and was half-way through an industrial-size popcorn.

Players warmed up on the ice. The red and white uniforms of the Dinos circled one half of the rink, while Edmonton's green and gold university team shot pucks at their goalie at the other end.

"Hey, look at that." Matt pointed across the rink. His right arm came up a little too quickly. He spilled some popcorn.

The Dinos' mascot, a red-and-white dinosaur named Rex, stood behind the crowd and did a series of cartwheels. The antics were made all the more amazing because of Rex's tail. It was at least as long as he was tall.

Lane watched Arthur beaming and enjoying Matt's company. Matt pointed again. Lane's eyes followed.

Two men in masks ran along the aisle behind Rex. Both wore latex masks—presidential caricatures, Lane realized—running shoes, and Speedos. The crowd was momentarily silent. One president looped a necklace the size of a Hula-Hoop around Rex's neck. Lane stared at what was attached to the front of the necklace.

"It's a dildo!" a fan said.

When he spotted the pair of presidents, Rex turned to the right. The dildo swung a millisecond later.

"Rex's got a dick around his neck!" another fan said.

Hearing his name called, Rex swung to the left. The dildo stopped at the top of its arc, then flopped back around. The crowd roared with laughter.

A camera flashed.

Lane headed for the door followed by Matt and Arthur. *The presidential impersonators will be headed for the parking lot,* he thought.

Outside, Lane watched a vintage Lincoln race out of the parking lot.

"That them?" Matt asked.

Lane looked at Matt.

Arthur looked worried as he stood behind the boy.

"Did you get the plate?" Arthur asked.

"Nope." Lane looked at Matt. "Did you?"

Matt said, "Too far away. How'd you know to look out here?"

"Think like the guys in the Speedos. They had to have planned an escape. So, just think ahead a bit."

Matt smiled, "Cool."

Lane looked at Arthur. A frown darkened Arthur's face.

"How about we go get something to eat?" Lane asked.

"I'm starved," Matt said.

"Good idea," Arthur said.

Matt's growing on me, Lane thought. *This could get complicated.*

+ + +

Matt was asleep on the couch. Arthur had covered the boy with his mother's quilt then promptly fallen asleep on the recliner.

Lane watched the TV. Text ran across the bottom of the screen. CNN was describing the latest US military adventure. A reporter wearing a kevlar helmet stood in front of a tank.

The phone rang.

Lane picked it up right away, hoping it wouldn't wake the sleepers. "Hello?"

"It's me," Harper said.

Arthur snored.

"What's that?" Harper asked.

"Arthur's asleep." Lane kept his voice low so as not to wake him.

Harper laughed. "Hope you two have separate bedrooms. Sounds like a freight train. Look, I just got a couple of interesting calls. Thought you'd want to know."

"Go."

"I called Bobbie's church. The minister called me back about an hour ago. He went on for fifteen minutes about how Bobbie was his idol. Kept calling her a saint. Ever since Bobbie's name went up on the sign outside of the church, it's been packed on Sundays. Did I mention that he said she was a saint?"

Lane said, "Go on."

Harper said, "Here's where it gets interesting. About twenty minutes after that, I got a call from a woman. She must have been calling from a pay phone, because there was the sound of traffic in the background. She told me to check into a resort in Jamaica. Said it might help me to find out the truth about Bobbie. She wouldn't leave a name and hung up when I asked for one."

Lane watched the muzzle flash of a tank on the television. "Won't hurt to check the resort out."

Arthur snored. Matt made it a duet.

"I wonder who it was who called from the pay phone?" Harper asked.

"My bet would be the minister's wife," Lane said.

Wednesday, October 14

Chapter 8

LANE DROVE UP the 14th Street hill south of 17th Avenue. He turned right, onto a street lined with apartments and four-plexes. Just across from Buckmaster Park was a four-suite apartment. To Lane, it looked early '50s, which the white stucco and green trim confirmed. He and Harper had divided up the interviews to save time. Harper was trying to find out if there was anything to yesterday's Jamaica tip.

Lane thought about the telephone conversation he'd had with Charles' sister. She'd said, "You come to my place and we'll talk. But you'd better be prepared to listen."

He walked up to the door then downstairs to her apartment. The moist scent of mould reached out to him. The woman who opened the door was a little taller than 150 centimetres. Her hair was somewhere between brown and blond. She had a round, no-nonsense face and might have been thirty or thirty-five. *But that was a week ago*, Lane thought. Grief had added a decade to her age.

"Are you Lane?" she asked.

Lane heard the exhaustion in her voice. He thought, *She's cried herself out.* "Yes, Ms. Reddie."

She took a deep breath before she said, "Call me Denise." She closed the door behind him, then pointed at the living room. "It's tiny. I like it that way."

There were two chairs in the room. Lane took one.

"I'm gonna have a cup of coffee. You want one?" Denise said.

Lane hesitated, then said, "Please."

"Cream and sugar?"

"Black," Lane said.

She shuffled back with a cup for each of them.

Lane took a sip. "Good stuff."

"Charles liked the way I made coffee. Aren't you gonna ask me any questions?" She sat across from him.

"You said you wanted me to listen."

"That's right," Denise said.

Lane waited.

Denise watched Lane for at least a minute before saying, "My brother had to work for everything he got. Bought an old welding rig and built up his business until he could afford a new truck. Then he built a house. Did a lot of the work himself or got friends to help out. That's the house Bobbie and Cole live in."

There was something about the way she said "Bobbie", Lane thought. It was a curse on Denise's lips.

"He and Bobbie met at my wedding." Denise laughed. It was laced with irony. "A bad omen. My marriage lasted for three years. Anyway, Charles and Bobbie got married six months later, and six months after that, Cole was born. Charles told me he was getting ready to break it off when they found out she was pregnant. After they got married, I saw less and less of Charles. Bobbie wanted him all to herself.

"Then, Charles got in touch with me a couple of

months ago. I hadn't heard from him in almost a year. He came over here and started crying. You see, Bobbie had gone to Jamaica with a bunch of fans from some radio-show contest. It was one of those deals where women phoned in to win a free trip to a resort. Apparently, that really helped Bobbie's ratings."

Lane leaned closer to hear all that Denise said. Tone of voice was crucial. She wasn't looking at Lane now. She was seeing her dead brother the day he had come to visit her months earlier.

"She went on her trip. Charles stayed home with the kids. They picked her up at the airport. Right in front of the kids she told Charles she'd found someone else. Told him she was going back to meet this guy—I think his name was Frank or something. Bobbie was bringing him back to Canada. And that was it for Charles, his kids, and the house he built."

"Did this Frank come to Canada?" Lane pulled out a notebook and began to write.

"No, Bobbie went back to Jamaica a week later. Returned alone. She acted all sorry. Said she wanted to patch things up with Charles, but he wasn't having any of it."

"What happened then?" Lane asked.

"Things got nasty."

+ + +

"How do you find these places?" Harper asked. He looked around. They were at the back of Colombian Coffee House. The white, eight-foot fence gave them plenty of privacy. They sat in green plastic chairs and sipped coffee. None of the other three tables were occupied. The owner was inside making their sandwiches.

"I don't know. I just keep my eyes open," Lane said.

"So, what did Charles' sister have to say?" Harper took a sip and looked at Lane over the rim of his cup.

"She said Bobbie wanted a divorce after she went on a trip to Jamaica. Met some guy named Frank. She went back to Jamaica to get Frank but came home alone. She wanted Charles back. When he said no way, she started making threats," Lane said.

"Like what?"

"Guess she kept it vague but Denise, Charles' sister, said Bobbie had Charles convinced the lives of his children were going to be hell if he didn't play by Bobbie's rules." Lane lifted his cup.

"You believe the sister?"

"She was pretty convincing. Seemed to be very careful about sticking to what she saw and heard. The funny thing was she didn't try to convince me that Charles couldn't have killed his daughter. I kept expecting her to say it. The way she talked about Charles, it was obvious she thought he was not a killer. But she never came out and said he didn't do it. It was very odd," Lane said.

"Here you go." The owner slid two plates onto the table. They were stacked with kettle-bread sandwiches skewered with toothpicks.

"Looks good," Harper picked up half a turkey sandwich.

"Always is," Lane said.

"Enjoy." The owner went back inside.

"That's not the only odd thing," Harper said.

Lane didn't talk. Instead, he chewed a mouthful of sandwich.

"I checked out the trip to Jamaica. It was the last week in July. One of those radio promotions where the twelfth caller wins a trip. Bobbie went with about 120 other women on an all-expenses-paid vacation to a singles resort." Harper waited for a reaction from Lane.

Lane put his right hand over his mouth, chewed, and shrugged.

"Man, you've got a swinger living next door, and you don't know it. I mention singles resort, and you don't get it."

Lane swallowed before he said, "Get what?"

"An all female trip. Singles resorts often hire buff guys to work the resorts. Some women go just to get the "big bamboo" and a tan." Harper shook his head in frustration with Lane's bewilderment. "Do I have to draw you pictures?"

"You mean?" Lane was beginning to get the picture.

"Some women go to singles resorts for a sex holiday. Denise's story jives with what I found out. Bobbie did return to the resort for a week in August. I've made a series of calls. The resort staff puts me on hold, or someone takes a message, then no one gets back to me. I've been playing a marathon game of telephone tag."

"Why would they avoid you?" Lane asked.

"I'm not sure. It's not likely I'll get a ticket to fly

down there to find out. I'm gonna have to get the information some other way."

"Did you try the local police?" Lane's phone rang. He flipped it open. "Hello."

"Can you meet me at Matt's school?" Arthur asked. There was panic in his voice.

"Is he okay?" Lane asked.

"He's been suspended. The principal wants us to come to school. We made an appointment for three o'clock. Said he wants both of us there," Arthur said.

"But we have no legal rights here," Lane said.

"Yes we do. Martha signed a form so I could get Matt into school. We're in the process of becoming Matt's guardians."

Lane took a quick breath. He thought about asking, "When were you going to let me in on this?" Instead, he said, "Three o'clock. Where?"

Arthur told him.

"I'll be there," Lane said.

+ + +

Matt's school was located off Macleod Trail. Its massive concrete walls stood two stories and held more than 2500 students. A car, carrying four teens, peeled out of the parking lot. The driver spotted the unmarked police car, backed his foot off the accelerator, and drove by without making eye contact.

Harper glared as they passed. He dropped Lane off near the front doors. Inside the school, Lane met Arthur in the main foyer. Students passed by. One of the younger ones almost knocked Lane flat with a backpack weighing nearly half the boy's body weight.

"What's it about?" Lane asked.

Arthur dodged a young woman with more cleavage than a movie star at an awards ceremony. "He called his English teacher an asshole."

Lane began to answer, thought better of it, and followed Arthur.

They opened the door of the office. A pair of students sat in chairs to their left. Matt was one of them. Lane noted that the boy's face reflected a mix of anger and dread. Lane sat down next to him and said, "What happened?"

Matt shook with anger. "The teacher asked us about revenge. I told the class a story. The teacher made fun of me, and I called him an asshole. I hate bein' treated like that!" He looked at the wall as if resigned to the inevitable lecture.

Arthur sat down on the other side.

Lane put the thumb and forefinger of his right hand against his forehead. Matt twitched his shoulders and ducked.

"Nobody's going to hit you," Lane said.

Matt looked back at him as if to say, "We'll see."

Arthur nodded at Lane and mouthed, "Go ahead."

"Start from the top. Tell us everything that happened," Lane said.

"The teacher asked if anyone had a story to tell about revenge, so I put my hand up. I explained what I did to Phil." Matt looked from Lane to Arthur.

"Phil's a cousin," Arthur said.

"Keep going," Lane said.

"We went to a family reunion one weekend. It was out in the country. Sunday morning we went to church. Halfway through, Phil needed to go to the bathroom. He'd been buggin' me all weekend, sayin' stuff about the way I walk and gettin' me into trouble, so I took him outside, and showed him where to go." Matt looked a little unsure if he should continue.

"Go on," Lane said.

"I told him, 'If you piss on the fence it'll turn to steam.' He did what I said, and started screaming. Then, he pissed all down the front of his pants."

"I don't understand," Lane said.

"The fence was electrified," Matt said as if every other human on the face of the planet knew that. "Everybody in the church rushed out. Aunt Margaret smacked me a couple of good ones up against the side of the head. Dad gave me a couple more."

"You were kicked out of class because you told the story?" Arthur was more than a little bewildered.

"No, the kids loved it. They all laughed. It was Mr. Smith," Matt said.

"Tell us the rest." Lane tried not to smile. He was only partly successful.

Matt said, "After everyone stopped laughing, Mr. Smith said, 'Anyone got another rootin' tootin' cow-poke revenge story?'"

Lane looked at Arthur in confusion.

Matt said, "It was the way he said it. All sarcastic

like. I told you I hate it when people treat me like I'm some kinda freak."

"Oh." Lane stopped smiling.

"You're here to see Mr. Todd?" a woman behind the counter asked. Her red hair sprung out around her head like steel wool.

"That's us," Arthur said.

"Come with me." She led them along a hallway to a conference room. "He'll be right in." She closed the door behind her.

"What are you gonna do?" Matt asked.

"I don't know. Listen to what they have to say, I guess. After that, we all need to sit down and talk when we get home." Lane looked at Arthur for support.

Arthur said, "That's right."

The door opened. A woman stepped in. "I'm Mrs. Stuckart. Something's come up. The principal asked me to talk with you. I'm Matt's administrator."

Lane noted that the woman almost looked them in the eye even though they were sitting. She had a round figure and wore glasses. Lane watched her eyes taking the measure of the three of them. *Don't underestimate her,* he thought.

Mrs. Stuckart sat down across from them, "Mr. Lane and Mr. Mereli, you're in the process of obtaining legal guardianship of Matt?"

"That's correct." Arthur didn't look at Lane.

"We've got a letter on file from Matt's mother. How is she?" Mrs. Stuckart asked.

Matt studied the faces of the adults around the table.

"Fine," Arthur said.

"You can stop pretending. I know she's got cancer. I'm not stupid." Matt's voice broke.

Arthur's mouth dropped open.

Lane studied Matt with growing respect.

Arthur cleared his throat. "She's at the Tom Baker Cancer Centre." Sweat rolled down the sides of his face.

"Do you three need time to talk?" Mrs. Stuckart asked.

Lane said, "If we started now, I suspect we'd be busy till midnight. We'd best deal with the suspension first."

"Matt and I have talked already, and I've asked Mr. Smith to join us," she said.

Lane detected something in her tone when she said "Mr. Smith." The name appeared to give her indigestion.

There was a knock on the door. Mr. Smith came in, and Lane felt the anger rising from Matt like heat on an August highway.

After introductions, Mr. Smith sat at the head of the table. Lane studied the man's smile, his trendy haircut, the way faux friendliness was not reflected in his eyes.

Lane decided the time for listening had passed. "We're going to talk with Matt about his choice of words. His reaction was not appropriate, but I'd like to ask Mr. Smith about his teaching style." Lane looked at Mrs. Stuckart. He noted a brief, almost imperceptible smile cross her lips. Lane looked at Smith. "Would you recommend sarcasm in dealing with young people?"

"Of course not," Smith said.

"Matt doesn't react well to sarcasm," Lane said.

Mr. Smith said, "I'm sorry if I gave Matt the impression I was being sarcastic. It was entirely unintentional." He smiled.

Lane thought, *I don't believe a word of it.*

"Do you believe in family values?" Mr. Smith's voice was ripe with ridicule.

Arthur pushed his chair back and stood. "This meeting's over." Arthur looked at Mrs. Stuckart. "My nephew is not going back into this man's class."

Lane and Matt started to follow. Arthur was already out the door.

+ + +

Matt broke the five-minute silence from the back seat of the Jeep. "What was that family values thing all about?" They were halfway home, and stuck in traffic on Glenmore Trail. On either side of the causeway, the reservoir water reflected sunlight.

Lane saw the sweat breaking out on Arthur's forehead.

Here we go, Lane thought.

"Lane and I are gay. Mr. Smith was trying to intimidate us. Family values was a thinly-veiled insult," Arthur said.

Lane heard fear of rejection in Arthur's voice. Memories of former judgments and rejection by the vast majority of the members of Arthur's family laced each word. Lane knew Arthur's coming-out had been a nightmare of recriminations.

"Oh, I already know you're gay." Matt's tone made it clear that he was far smarter than both the old men in the front seat. "I just don't know how Smith knew it."

"Well, he phrased it like a threat. The tone in his voice was unmistakable," Lane said.

"That's why I called him an asshole. That's the way he talked to me," Matt said.

"So, Mrs. Stuckart is going to get you out of Smith's class," Arthur said.

Matt said, "Guys like Smith don't go away. They're like my dad. They always find ways to make you pay."

"Your dad's a long way away," Lane said.

"Half the kids in this school belong to the same church as my dad. He's closer than you think. That's how Smith knew about you."

"So, what do you want us to do?" Arthur asked.

"Take me to see my Mom," Matt said.

+ + +

BOBBIE: Good afternoon. It's Bobbie on the ride home. I'd like to thank all of my listeners for the kind words, thoughts, and prayers. Today's program is about grief and living with it. What do I do after the funeral is over and my child's room is empty? How can God fill up my life? Brenda, you're caller number one.

BRENDA: I want to know how you stop hating your ex! I mean, he killed your baby girl!

BOBBIE: I don't know. I protected the children as best I could. Other women in my situation know the laws in this country make it difficult. After my husband left, his behaviour became more and more violent. I blame myself for not seeing this coming. *Bobbie took a long, shuddering breath.*

+ + +

Jay and Tony sat beside one another sipping coffee from white cups. They relaxed in front of the university library where the grassy courtyard was being sucked clean by a green four-wheeled vacuum the size of a dumpster.

Jay said, "It would be better if we waited a little longer. Let Rex get a little complacent." He looked nervously at the machine. The noise meant the volume of their conversation was dangerously loud.

Tony took a thoughtful sip of coffee. He wore black today and drank his coffee the same way. "Did you ever notice that when you fart, a girl will always come up to talk with you? And it seems like the intensity of the odour is directly correlated with the level of attraction or repulsion to the female."

"You're starting to sound like a professor. Too may lectures are rotting your brain." A noxious stench reached Jay. "And that's not all that's rotting!"

"Tony?" the young woman asked. Her hair was black, reaching to the base of her spine. She wore a red blouse and white slacks.

Jay felt like singing and hoped for a gust of wind to clear the air. *She is stunning,* he thought. *I never thought I'd feel like this after what my sister did to me.*

Tony said, "Rosie, this is Jay. What's up?"

"Besides the fact that you stink!" Rosie turned up her nose with disgust.

Jay's heart sank. She wasn't going to stick around for long.

"It runs in the family," Tony said.

"Uncle Tran wants the family to get together for dinner on Sunday at The Lucky Elephant and he wants Jay to come too." Rosie smiled at Jay.

"Okay." Tony looked at Jay. "You coming?"

If Rosie's going to be there, Jay thought. "Sure."

"See you there." Rosie walked away.

Jay watched the way her body moved and fought the urge to write poetry. "She's your cousin?"

"Yep. The real thing. Mom's brother is Rosie's father." Tony smiled.

"What's so funny?" Jay asked.

"You're red in the face." Tony began to laugh.

"How come I'm invited?"

"You know Uncle Tran. He's always on the lookout for orphans. It's his mission in life," Tony said.

Friday, October 16

Chapter 9

HARPER ASKED, "ISN'T this a bit paranoid?"

They looked across the river at Bowness Park. Their car was parked at Baker Park on the north side of the Bow River. On this side, the remaining leaves were fading reds, yellows, and oranges.

"It's quiet here. It's what Lisa asked for." Lane wore a blue jacket over his sports coat. He yawned, and it made his jaw pop.

"You look like hell."

"No sleep." *The nightmares are starting up again,* Lane thought.

"Care to elaborate?" Harper leaned against the passenger door.

"After the meeting at the school, we went to see Martha." *In an hour or two I won't be so tired,* Lane thought, *I just need caffeine and some fresh air.* He opened his window.

"How is she doing?"

"Worse than I thought. I mean, it was the first time I've met the woman. She's got those sunken eyes. You've seen cancer patients before?"

"Oh, no," Harper said.

"Exactly. Matt was pretty shocked. I had to take him outside while Martha and Arthur talked. She wants us to have permanent custody of Matt, if the treatment doesn't work. According to her, Matt's dad is abusive. With the new wife and baby, Matt won't have much of a life with his father," Lane said.

"How old is Matt?"

"Fifteen," Lane said.

"You've got that deer-in-the-headlights expression." Harper chuckled.

"It's not funny." Lane began to smile all the same.

"Sure it is. There's nothing like a kid to upset your cozy little home. Your entire civilized little world is about to be turned upside down."

"You ought to know," Lane said.

"That's right, and you know what?"

"What?" Lane asked.

"It's worth it," Harper said.

"You don't understand. The kid began telling me things. Matt's father told him he was a freak and that it runs in Martha's family. It was a reference to Arthur and me and about Matt's disability. You see I'm sure Matt has CP (cerebral palsy). It looks like it's mild, but you can see it in the way he moves, and the way he concentrates when he walks."

"It's messy, isn't it? You're going through the adjustment phase. Erinn and I went through it when Glenn moved in. How's Arthur handling all of this?" Harper asked with a smile.

"We haven't talked much. It feels like I'm along for the ride, while he makes the decisions. I don't even think he's noticed the kid has CP!" Lane said.

"Look, as soon as Glenn started to live with us Erinn and I had to be on the same page or we were sunk. Sit Arthur down and talk."

"Martha made Arthur promise that if she dies we'll take care of Matt. Can you imagine how crazy it could get?" Lane asked.

"Yes, I do. Some people in my family haven't spoken with me since we took Glenn in. And for once, I know more about something than you do."

"A lot more than I know about this stuff. Now you've got a baby on the way. You're on your way to becoming an expert."

"Scary, isn't it?" Harper asked.

"Very," Lane said.

"Answer one thing."

"What?" Lane asked.

"Do you like the kid?"

"Yes."

Harper said. "Good. You didn't have to think about the answer. Besides, the kid will be sixteen soon, then he gets to decide where he wants to live. Erinn and I had to learn all those legal details when Glenn moved in."

An RCMP cruiser pulled up on Harper's side. He opened his window.

Lisa shifted into park before opening her window.

Lane noticed she was in uniform.

"Your place or mine?" Harper asked.

Lisa looked across at Lane. "You look like hell."

Lane studied her tone of voice. All business. Lisa saved this tone for the worst news. He thought, *this day is only going to get worse.* "Thanks for noticing. How about we walk?"

They walked the paved trail running alongside the river. A few leaves rattled in the trees. Those on the ground crunched underfoot. The river moved in the opposite direction and chuckled over submerged rocks.

Harper said, “Did you two ever stop to think that maybe you don’t need to keep hiding anymore? I mean you’ve known each other for years. You even have each other over for dinner. Maybe nobody cares.”

Lane and Lisa looked at Harper like he had said something stupid. “Things haven’t changed that much, especially in this province,” Lane said.

“Charles Reddie died of an allergic reaction to penicillin, not from carbon monoxide poisoning,” Lisa said.

“And no fingerprints on the duct tape,” Lane said.

Lisa said, “That’s correct. Also, the child had an unusual mark high up on her left thigh. We’ve got a photograph if you want to look. I showed the photo to some of the guys. One said it looked similar to an indentation he’d seen before. A body was stored in the trunk of a car. The mark may have been caused by what’s used to fasten down spare tires in late-model DaimlerChrysler products. We’re trying to find out if the fibres found on Kaylie’s pants are used to carpet DaimlerChrysler vehicles. We’re almost certain her upper body was wrapped in a garbage bag.”

“So, Kaylie’s body could have been driven to the campsite,” Harper said.

A pair of joggers passed them. The police officers waited before continuing the conversation.

"That would explain why Kaylie's runners were clean." Lane recalled Cole's immaculate white socks.

"One other thing. There was a cigarette butt on the cushion next to Kaylie's head. It had burned down to the filter, but the cushion didn't ignite. It had been treated with a fire retardant," Lisa said.

There was the sound of an outboard motor. Lisa turned right along a chainlink fence and away from the river. Behind them, the fire department's patrol boat roared up the river.

"Too many inconsistencies," Lane said.

"So, the investigation will have to remain open," Harper said.

"That's right," Lisa said.

They walked a narrow path lined by trees planted in parallel rows. The evergreens reached up more than thirty metres.

"It's funny," Harper said.

"No it's not," Lisa said.

"No, you don't understand. I got a fax this morning from the police in Jamaica. There was a fire at a resort during Bobbie's second trip. Two sisters and a GO died of smoke inhalation. The police attributed the fire to careless smoking," Harper said.

"GO?" Lisa asked.

"Guest organizer," Harper said.

"Gigolo?" Lisa asked.

"You catch on fast," Harper said.

"Do you have the names of the victims?" Lane asked.

"Not yet."

"We'll need them and any other details that might help," Lisa said.

"Keep in touch." Lane smiled at Lisa.

"I hear you've got an addition to the family." Lisa smiled back. Her tone softened. "Arthur and Loraine talked on the phone. She said he's really excited about having his nephew staying there."

"And that's not the half of it. We'll have you and Loraine over when things settle down a bit," Lane said.

Their feet crunched over the uneven gravel in the parking lot. Lane studied the fender liners of their Chevy. He remembered what he'd seen coating the wheel wells of Bobbie's Chrysler. "You know, Bobbie's place is maybe ten minutes away."

After saying goodbye to Lisa, Harper drove north up Nose Hill Drive. "I forgot to tell you, some vet has been calling. Wants to see us. Says it's important. She keeps leaving messages."

"That's it, nothing more?" Lane asked.

"That's it."

"We need to get a look at Bobbie's car," Lane said.

"How are we gonna do that without a warrant or naming her as a suspect?" Harper asked.

"We could ask her."

Harper pulled up to the red light near Crowchild Trail. "Maybe she's not even home. She's probably at the radio station."

"She does an afternoon show. Let's give it a try. Do a quick check as we drive by. I remember seeing something the first day we went to meet with Bobbie."

"What's that?" The light turned green. Harper pulled ahead.

"The day I was sick, Bobbie's car was freshly cleaned and waxed, but there was dust stuck to the wheel wells. It looked a lot like the dust stuck on this car after we drove out to see the bodies of Charles and Kaylie."

"Why didn't you say so?" Harper looked across at his partner.

"I didn't think of it until just a few minutes ago."

Within five minutes, they approached Bobbie's house.

"That doesn't look like her car in the driveway," Harper said.

"It's a new Acura," Lane said.

"About fifty-thousand dollars worth of automobile," Harper said.

Both looked at the black two door gleaming on Bobbie's driveway. The rear license plate read SPK 2ME.

+ + +

Harper clicked the mouse. They sat in a borrowed office in the Silver Springs District Office. Lane sat next to him and studied the screen. Harper said, "She got the Acura yesterday. The news on the Chrysler is unusual, though. Looks like it was scrapped."

"But it was only two years old."

"You wanna check out the junkyards or phone the vet?" Harper asked.

Ten minutes later, they drove down John Laurie

Boulevard. The sign at Bobbie's church had a new message: *I won't fall to pieces, I'll just fall at the feet of my Saviour.* Lane read it and recalled the look on Cole Reddie's face when he heard the news of his sister's death.

+ + +

"How come you never listen to the radio?" Tony asked. After their last class, rush-hour traffic on Crowchild Trail was just beginning to build.

"There's so much crap on the radio." Jay turned up the music. "We'll be early for work. Wanna grab a slurpee?"

"Don't change the subject. I've never once been in this car when you listened to the radio. You've always got your own music on. And, come to think of it, I've never seen you read a newspaper." Tony leaned against the passenger door and studied his friend.

Jay looked over at Tony, "Fuck! I hate the papers! I hate the radio! Isn't that good enough for you?"

Tony looked ahead, "Okay. If you don't wanna talk about it, you don't wanna talk about it. Man, we used to be able to talk about anything. Maybe you need to talk to Bobbie on the radio for advice."

"Shut up!" Jay's face was lipstick red.

"Okay man, have it your way. You still comin' for dinner on Sunday? Uncle Tran doesn't invite everybody, you know."

Jay took a deep breath and thought about Rosie.

"Rosie'll be there. Don't worry. I saw the way you looked at her," Tony said.

"What the hell's your problem?" Jay felt like Tony was reading his mind.

"You know what?" Tony asked.

"What?" Jay pretended to study the road.

"She was watchin' you pretty close too."

+ + +

BOBBIE: Good afternoon. It's Bobbie on the ride home. Friday's here, and the weekend's looking good. Let's talk about renewal. Doing something nice for me. You know, taking care of the one who cares for everyone else. Come on callers, what do you do to put a smile on your face? I could use some help.

+ + +

"I like this kind of fall day," Harper said.

"No bugs," Lane said as they pulled onto the gravel lot and parked in front of Idaho Metals. The sky was clear. The temperature was twenty degrees Celsius. The Idaho Metals office was a single-wide trailer in front of a six-foot chain-link fence topped with three strands of barbed wire.

Inside, they were greeted by a woman, maybe thirty years old, who looked up at them as they entered. "Cops," she said under her breath.

"Detectives Lane and Harper." Lane looked at her, sensed anxiety, and decided a change in approach might be the best way to go. He spotted a photograph on her desk. "Twins?"

"Yep. It's an old picture. They're ten now," she said.

Lane looked at her left hand and, seeing no rings, said, "It's tough raising kids these days." Lane read the triangular sign on her desk. "It's Joan isn't it?"

"That's right. And, I'm lucky. They're good boys. How can I help you?" She stood.

Lane spotted the sweat stains under her arms. *It's not that hot in here,* he thought. "We're looking for information on a late-model Chrysler owned by Bobbie Reddie."

"I see." Joan swallowed.

Harper looked at Lane, then back at Joan.

"Could you tell us anything about its present location or status?" Lane asked.

"You'd have to ask Mike. He's out in the yard. Just go out the door and walk through the gate."

The yard was a maze of wrecked cars, through knee-high grass and weeds. The hum of traffic on the freeway was constant.

"She was getting a little nervous," Harper said.

"That's for sure," Lane said.

"Wonder what she has to feel guilty about?" Harper asked.

"I'm not sure. Maybe it has something to do with the car and maybe not. So, it's Mike we're looking for, right?" Lane walked next to Harper between rows of cars. Those with damaged back ends were usually missing hoods, grills, and bumpers. A few were missing engines. One sat with its entire front end removed right up to the firewall.

At the end of the row, a man in blue coveralls sat

inside the engine compartment of a pale-blue pickup. One of his boots was propped on a fender. He wore a ball cap with its brim pointing backward.

A cellphone rang.

Lane and Harper looked at one other, wondering whose cell was ringing.

"Hello," the man in the coveralls said. "Yeah we got one of those. It's near the fence, on the north side of the shredder. The windshield's good." He listened for a moment then looked at Lane and Harper. "They're here."

"Mike?" Lane asked.

"Yep." Mike flipped the phone shut. He rested his nose on the back of his right wrist.

Harper leaned on the fender of the truck. Lane stood next to the side mirror. It was leaning at an odd angle because one of the brackets was broken. He watched Mike's face.

The silence stretched out before anyone spoke.

"You remember a champagne-coloured, late-model Chrysler brought here by Bobbie Reddie?" Harper asked.

"Yep," Mike said, then waited.

"Look," Harper said, "we're just here for information."

Mike smiled and nodded a couple of times as if to say, "Sure you are."

Lane noted the wariness behind Mike's blue eyes, and the sense of humour revealed by the crow's feet. The man was clean-shaven, and his fingers looked like they had been turning wrenches for most of the last two decades. Lane said, "You want to get out of there? It doesn't look too comfortable."

Mike said, "I'll get out of here when I get this goddamned alternator out. Ask your frickin' questions."

"We need to know where the car is," Harper said.

Mike pointed at a mountain of shredded metal at the end of a conveyor belt. "In there."

"You shredded a new car?" Lane asked.

"She came in here sayin' she wanted her car shredded. Started cryin'. Said it was her way of gettin' rid of bad memories. We tried to talk her out of it. Then Joan, she's the secretary, pulled me over and said, 'The woman just lost her little girl.' So we took the serial numbers, drained the gas tank, took out the battery, and did as she asked. Then, Bobbie left."

"Did you salvage anything else from the car?" Lane asked.

"Just the tires." Mike lifted his cap, revealing a receding hairline.

"What happened to those?" Harper looked hopefully at Lane.

"One of the guys grabbed them. The tires had quite a bit of wear left, so he put 'em on his car. Nice wheels," Mike said.

"Did you wonder at all about her request?" Lane asked.

Mike chuckled, "The whole thing was weird. New car. Grieving mother who cried a lot. She stopped cryin' like someone had turned off a tap, when we agreed to do what she wanted. By the time she left, she was grinnin' from ear to ear. Either it was grief, or there was something freaky goin' on."

"Like what?" Lane asked.

"Well nothin' adds up. She cries about being all alone and losing a child. Says she doesn't know what she's gonna do now that she's a single mom. Then she shreds a car worth more than $15,000. We pay her nothin' for it. We make so much per-tonne on the scrap. She doesn't care. 'Just take care of it,' she says. When bits of metal start comin' out of the shredder, she's gets this big shit-eatin' grin on her face. If she's so grief-stricken and broke, how come she's smilin' from ear to frickin' ear? It just doesn't add up."

"You're right," Harper said.

"How's that?" Mike asked.

"It doesn't add up," Harper said.

Sure it does, Lane thought. As they walked away, he said to Harper, "We're not getting the whole story here."

Fifteen minutes later, Harper drove down Blackfoot Trail. The plan was to scoot around the Stampede Grounds and then downtown. "So, if we can't get the car, it rules out a fibre match. Now, we can't even look at the dirt stuck in the tire treads. The guy who got the tires could have driven anywhere."

"You're beginning to think Bobbie is a suspect?" Lane said.

"It's a definite possibility. I just don't want to exclude all suspects other than Bobbie." Harper glimpsed symmetrical rows of seats in the Stampede Grandstand on their right.

Lane smiled. "Point well taken."

"We could stop in and pay her a visit. The radio station is maybe ten minutes away."

"All right." Lane was quiet the rest of the way.

"I was wrong, it took eleven." Harper parked in front of Bobbie's radio station located near the river.

They walked through the revolving front doors of the cable TV and radio station. Ten storeys above their heads, a skylight illuminated the foyer.

Harper made eye contact with Lane and cocked his head, "Look at that."

Lane turned to see the flowers, stuffed animals, and white crosses arranged around a framed photograph of Kaylie Reddie.

Harper walked over to the security guard who stood behind a semicircle of countertop on a raised platform. Harper looked up at him, "We're here to see Ms. Reddie."

Lane pulled out his identification and showed it to the guard.

The guard wore a grey shirt, black tie, and a matching frown. He put his hands on his hips, "I'll have to call upstairs." He looked to his right and up the stairs.

"We'd rather you didn't," Lane said.

The guard smirked. "If I wanna keep my job, I'm gonna have to call." The guard lifted his chin and looked over Lane's shoulder.

Lane turned and spotted the red-carpeted stairway

leading to the second floor. He turned to Harper who was smiling at the guard.

The guard leaned across the counter and whispered, "Do I have to draw you guys a map? I need this job. The number one rule around here is don't mess with Bobbie. The best I can do is give you a head start!"

Leaning back, the guard picked up the phone and raised his voice. "I'm gonna call her right now. You two had better wait!"

"We'll just head upstairs," Harper said.

The guard said, "You'd better stop right there!"

Lane looked left. The eyes of at least twenty people were following Lane and Harper as they made their way upstairs.

The guard's voice chased them, "Two policemen are on their way up to see Ms. Reddie!"

Harper looked back and smiled.

At the top of the stairs, they stepped onto a tiled floor. The hallway was lined with life-sized portraits of singers. One poster watched them from the end of the hall. It took up an entire wall. Bobbie's image smiled at them. The caption said, *Talk to me!*

Overhead speakers carried the sounds of a radio show in progress. Lane recognized Bobbie's voice. He concentrated on the conversation.

CALLER: I know it's not today's topic but I'm worried about my daughter. Things are getting pretty intense with her and her boyfriend.

BOBBIE: I've got a suggestion. Does your daughter like Oreos?

CALLER: Loves them.

BOBBIE: Tomorrow morning, sit her down at the kitchen table.

CALLER: She's stays out late and sleeps in.

BOBBIE: Get her up early. Bring out the milk and Oreos.

CALLER: Okay.

BOBBIE: Offer her an Oreo, but before you hand it to her, open the cookie and lick the filling. Then put it back together. Hand it to her. When she says, "Yuck!" say, "Nobody wants a girl who loses her virginity."

CALLER: Thanks, Bobbie.

Lane and Harper stood on the outside of a wall of glass. Bobbie sat behind a desk the size of a small car and in front of a microphone. She was dressed in white.

Across from Bobbie, behind another glass wall, sat the producer. Bobbie's producer looked to be twenty-five years old and weighed maybe fifty kilograms. Lane watched for a reaction. There was none.

BOBBIE: I'll be back after a short break.

Harper knocked on the glass.

Bobbie looked up and stared at the officers.

The producer opened the glass door to Lane's left.

Lane and Harper stepped inside.

Bobbie glared at her producer.

"Hello Ms. Reddie," Lane said.

"I'm very busy." Bobbie leaned forward, blinking several times.

"There is one question." Lane moved closer. Harper moved to his right.

Bobbie leaned back. She looked behind the detectives.

"We've just come from Idaho Metals. We wondered what made you decide to shred your car?"

Bobbie wiped at her eyes. She looked beyond Harper and Lane.

Harper looked over his shoulder and said to Lane, "We've got an audience."

Lane focused on Bobbie's eyes.

"Have you ever lost a child?" Bobbie's voice wavered.

Lane thought, *She's playing me and whoever's behind me.* "We're here about the car."

"Just what are you accusing me of? I've lost my child! I'm the victim here!" Bobbie stood up. She pointed at the door. "I've got nothing to hide!"

Lane sensed that Bobbie was performing for an audience. He turned and saw the glass wall lined with faces. Not one of them was smiling. Lane looked left at the producer. She looked back at him with the same neutral expression she'd greeted him with earlier.

Five minutes later, Harper drove toward the centre of downtown. "That went well."

"I know you think it didn't." Lane watched a young woman skateboarding down the sidewalk. She weaved her way around and between pedestrians.

"You think it did?"

"Why wouldn't she answer the question?" Lane asked.

Harper thought for a minute. "A shredded car rules out a fibre match. It also means we can't even look at the dirt stuck in the wheel wells."

"So, Bobbie's covering?"

Harper checked the rear-view mirror. "It's a definite possibility. As I said, I just don't want to exclude all suspects other than Bobbie. Anything you want me to keep my eyes out for over the weekend?"

"If you want something to do, see if they can fax more of the details about the Jamaica fire. If you want a laugh, come and see me at referee school."

"You're joking," Harper said.

"I wish."

"Man, before you know it you'll be a hockey dad!"

"Not even a remote chance of that," Lane said.

Saturday, October 17

Chapter 10

IT FEELS GOOD *to be back on the ice, Lane thought, even though I haven't had time to buy new skates.*

The ancient figure skates had raised a few eyebrows. So had the black-and-white helmet he'd borrowed from Harper. The rookie referees spent the morning in class learning the rules of the game. Tomorrow, if he passed the test with an eighty-five percent or better, he would be a referee.

"The key to doing the job well is being at the right place all of the time." Bob was a referee with some international experience. Bob took pains to look the part with a short-short haircut covered by a black helmet with a visor. He wore a black-nylon sweatsuit. He was shorter than Lane and had quick feet and a sarcastic disposition. "Hey toe picks? Show me the best position for a referee if the players are crowded around the net and the puck is loose."

Lane took a couple of quick strides, reversed so his eyes would still be on the play, and positioned himself to one side behind the net. "Here."

"Right." Bob didn't bother to hide his disappointment. Lane was in perfect position. "Be sure to get a pair of hockey skates before your first game."

Lane opened his mouth to reply, then thought better of it. His cellphone chirped.

Bob frowned.

Lane picked the phone out of his pocket. He skated toward the penalty box. “Hello.”

“Hey Mr. Hockey, havin’ fun yet?” Harper said.

“Remind me I’ve got to get some new skates.” Lane leaned against the boards.

“Tell me you’re not out there with a pair of figure skates! You said you’d get new skates if I loaned you the helmet. You might as well hang a ‘pick-on-me’ sign around your neck.”

“No time to buy skates. Between the case, the hospital, and going to Matt’s school, there hasn’t been any time.” Lane looked over his shoulder at the other refs in training.

“Just got off the phone with the chief,” Harper said.

Bob blew his whistle. The sound echoed off the arena rafters. Lane stuck a finger in his left ear. He pressed the phone closer to his right.

“She asked how come we haven’t closed the Reddie case. So, I explained about the inconsistencies.”

“What did she say?” Lane asked.

“There’s been some pressure on her end. A few calls from concerned citizens who think Bobbie’s been through enough. They encouraged the chief to hurry it up and close this case since the father is obviously responsible.”

“Go on.”

“Chief seems to think the calls may have some political influence,” Harper said.

“City Hall?” Lane asked.

"And the legislature. Nothing that could be nailed down, otherwise it would become political interference. The calls did come from people who are well-connected, though." Harper chuckled.

"What's funny?"

"The chief can smell fish a long way off. Has a nose for it. This one is beginning to stink. She said to keep on it. If there's pressure to close this case, we may be on to something. The chief thinks the pressure might intensify."

"I wonder who's been whispering in the right ears?" Lane asked.

Harper said, "I was wondering the same thing. Oh, and make sure you read the paper today."

"What?"

"Read it. Talk to you later." Harper hung up.

It was after six by the time Lane arrived home. He anticipated that he'd feel some pain when he put the skates back on in the morning. The house was unusually quiet. Riley slept in a tiny patch of sunlight on the front-room floor. He opened his eyes and wagged his tail when he spotted Lane. Arthur said, "Supper's in the fridge. We took the dog for a walk after we went to the hospital. Matt ate supper and went to bed. The kid's dead tired. And, by the look of things, so are you."

"What about you? Those pants of yours look like they're getting a little baggy." Lane pulled a salad plate and a beer from the fridge.

Arthur grabbed his belt and hitched up his pants, "If I'd known this would help me lose weight, I would've had a kid a long time ago."

"Did you read the paper?" Lane sat down.

Arthur shrugged. He looked even more tired. "This time it says that a woman like Bobbie Reddie shouldn't have to be put through a long investigation. According to the editorial, it's obvious the father killed the child and himself. Bobbie and her son have had more than enough of their share of pain and suffering."

"Sounds like someone's been busy. The chief's been getting calls."

"Oh?" Arthur asked.

"Harper called me." Lane stabbed at some salad, maneuvered it into his mouth, began to chew. "Some influential citizens have expressed their concerns to the chief. They want a quick resolution to this case."

"Could we talk about the case?" Arthur got up, reached into the fridge, and brought out a bottle of white wine.

"As long as we get to talk about Matt and what he's got on his plate." Lane pointed at Arthur with his fork.

"For instance?" Arthur's tone of voice was immediately defensive.

"CP for starters."

"What are you talking about?" Arthur looked through a drawer for the corkscrew. It sounded more like demolition than searching.

"Cerebral palsy. Look. I like the kid. I want him here. You want him here. No need to get defensive."

Arthur pulled out the corkscrew, and plunked it and the wine bottle in front of Lane. "So, what is the point?"

The corkscrew squeaked as Lane twisted it into the cork. "We need to talk about what's going on. You know, discuss things."

Arthur put two glasses on the table.

The cork popped out of the bottle. Lane said, "Like the fact that we haven't been discussing major decisions, and what are we going to do if Martha gets sicker? Things like that."

Arthur sat down and asked, "What makes you think he's got CP?"

Lane poured. "It's the way he moves. There's a hitch in his walk. Did you notice the way he holds his arm?"

"Shit." Tears welled-up in Arthur's eyes. "I thought he was just a little uncoordinated. I missed seeing the kid grow up, and I'm so far out of the loop no one bothered to tell me."

"Matt's dad called him a freak, and said it ran in Martha's family. It looks like the kid needs a place where he's accepted for who he is. Where nobody cares if he's got CP," Lane said.

"How the hell does he play goal?"

Lane shrugged, "I guess we're going to find out."

"You know, it's funny." Arthur looked at the legs of white wine running down the inside of his glass. "Martha told me that getting cancer was a blessing in some ways. She'd gotten used to being bullied by her husband. She even made excuses for the way he treated Matt. When Martha found out she had cancer, she told herself, 'No more.' She said she felt good about herself for the first time in years."

"So, what's she planning to do?" Lane asked.

"I helped her hire a lawyer. She's going after half of everything her husband owns."

"This could get messy," Lane said.

"No kidding. Speaking of messy, Mrs. Smallway is building a glass addition to her house. She was hollering at some poor guy in her backyard. It has to be done for Halloween. Apparently, she's having a few friends over for a party." Arthur smiled.

"You don't think it's another swinger's party?"

"I bet she's planning a costume ball," Arthur laughed.

"Scary."

"Very. Now, tell me more about the case," Arthur said.

Sunday, October 18

Chapter 11

AFTER WRITING AND passing his referee's examination, the newly qualified Lane drove west on Memorial Drive. He was first in line at the traffic lights more times than not. The sun shone just above the mountains in a blue sky. He caught glimpses of the river shimmering on his left. Orange and yellow leaves covered the banks and pathways. A few joggers and cyclists pursued their dinnertime workouts along the river.

After listening to Lane summarize the evidence, Arthur had said one thing last night that bothered Lane that next day. "You may never be able to prove it, but that's not the worst of it. If you're right, then Cole is a witness."

He looked left at Chinatown, then glanced at the clock. *I'll be home by seven,* he thought and continued along the north side of the river.

Seven o'clock, Uncle Tran said seven, Jay thought. He found a parking spot on the south side of the river, locked the car, and walked the rest of the way to the restaurant. Tony waved when Jay entered the door. There was a seat next to Tony's mother. It was across the table from Rosie and her father. Jay dodged toddlers who ran by as he wove his way around and between tables. He glanced up at the jade elephant before sitting down. Uncle Tran nodded at him from the next table.

"Glad you made it," Tony said.

His mother smiled. "Hello, Jay."

Jay offered his hand. She shook it with gentle affection.

"You, good boy." She turned to Tony and said something in Vietnamese.

"She says she wishes she knew more English," Tony said.

"I wish I knew more Vietnamese." Jay picked up a menu to hide behind, before he glanced across the table.

"Hi. This is my father, Hieng." Rosie wore a white blouse and a gold chain around her neck.

"Hello," Jay said, while thinking that Hieng must be close to sixty years old.

Hieng nodded at Jay.

Jay nodded back.

"My father is glad to meet you." Rosie used her elbow to jab her father in the ribs. Hieng smiled obediently.

The waiter arrived as soon as Jay set his menu down. He took a look around the restaurant and counted four empty chairs.

Food orders came and went. The air filled with the scent of noodles, chicken, beef, peanut sauce, peppers, ginger, curry, and salt.

"My Mom says you're our guest today," Tony said.

"Shouldn't I be paying?" Jay asked before remembering he only had enough money for some gas and one meal a day until payday. He had been dreaming about tonight's satay soup while studying in the university library.

Tony ignored his friend's offer. "On a day like today, all of the money is put into an account. If anyone here has to make an emergency trip to Vietnam, then this money is used."

"I should . . . " Jay began.

Rosie said, "Auntie is very stubborn. Just smile. Say thank you."

"Thank you," Jay said.

Tony's mother said something to her son. Tony said, "My mom asks why are you turning red?"

Who knows, Jay thought. Their orders arrived before he could be expected to answer.

He hardly looked up from the bowl. Jay used chopsticks to gather up noodles and fill his mouth.

The clatter of conversation and eating died away to a murmur. Jay looked up from what was left of his soup. A noodle reached from his lower lip to the bowl.

Tony's mother smiled at Jay when he slurped up the noodle and wiped his chin with a napkin.

Rosie giggled.

Jay looked left.

Uncle Tran was standing right next to him.

Uncle Tran put his arm on Jay's shoulder.

The restaurant was silent except for the voice of a toddler who said, "How are you? How ARE you! How are YOU!"

Even though he was sitting and Tran standing, Jay and Uncle Tran were nearly eye to eye.

Tran put a jeweller's box in front of Jay.

Jay looked at Tony for help.

"Open it," Tony said.

Jay found himself unable to speak. His fingers fumbled to open the box. In between two layers of white cotton, he saw a gold elephant on a gold chain.

Tony said, "Uncle Tran wants me to explain because you're my friend and you have watched out for me, treated me like an equal. If you put the elephant on, it means you've accepted us, all of us, as your family. In one way or another, we're all orphans, and you're being invited to join this family."

Jay's fingers fumbled with the clasp. He dropped the chain. Panic gripped him. Even the children were quiet now. Jay shoved his chair back, fighting the urge to run.

He glanced at Rosie who glared at him.

Jay picked up the chain.

His fingers refused to work.

There was the soft touch of a woman's hand on his. Jay looked up into the face of Tony's mother. He recognized the emotions of grief and love. She took the chain and opened the clasp. He felt the cold of the chain at his throat, and the warmth of her hands at the back of his neck. She closed the link then rested her hands on his shoulders.

Jay used his right hand to touch the elephant at his throat.

"You're family now," Tony said.

Monday, October 19

Chapter 12

"ARTHUR? HARPER JUST called. Things are really hopping. I'm meeting him for coffee. Are you and Matt going to be okay?" Lane was just out of the shower, and he noticed a few damp spots coming through the front of his shirt as he was knotting his tie.

"I'll drive Matt to school," Arthur said.

Matt sat eating cereal, across the table from Arthur. The boy nodded at Lane.

The phone rang.

Arthur reached for it. "Hello? Lisa. Yes, we're fine. It has been interesting. Yes, I'm sorry too, but . . . Lane's right here."

Lane took the phone. "Hello, Lisa."

"I just got a call from Dr. Fibre. You know, the forensics genius with absolutely no social skills. He looks like something out of a male model magazine but can't pick a pair of pants to match a shirt or tie," Lisa said.

"I met him once." Lane took a sip of coffee.

"He said he got some fibres off of Kaylie's clothing. A few were animal; canine. And some were consistent with the material used to carpet the trunks of late-model cars. He's confident he can make a match, if you can find the vehicle. Fibre confirmed that her upper body was wrapped in a plastic consistent with the material used to manufacture garbage bags."

Lisa sounded better today, more optimistic, Lane

thought. “The car’s a problem. Bobbie had her old car shredded. She’s already bought a new one.”

Lisa said, “The car was only a couple of years old. Sounds like a calculated move. Destroying evidence. Staying one step ahead of you.”

“Looks like it,” Lane said.

“Pretty damning when you think about it.”

“Damning but not the kind of evidence that would be damning in court,” Lane said.

“Probably not. I’ll keep you informed from this end. Something else may turn up.”

“I’ll keep you up-to-date on what we find,” Lane said.

“Good. Take care.” Lisa hung up.

Lane and Harper met twenty minutes later at a coffee shop on Kensington. A table by the window offered privacy.

Lane sipped a Rolo, with its delicious blend of espresso, chocolate and caramel.

Harper said, “We may have caught a break. Bobbie has a brother. Name’s Jay Krocker. He’s nineteen. Problem is there appears to be no fixed address. It may take a while to track him down. And get this, their parents died when Jay was fifteen. It was a house fire attributed to careless smoking. Jay claimed his parents had quit smoking. Still, the investigators couldn’t find a cause other than careless smoking. I’ve asked for the file so we can take a look.”

“That’s three,” Lane said.

“Three?” Harper asked.

“Two fires attributed to careless smoking and a

burned-out cigarette butt in the camper. It's beginning to look like a pattern." Lane stirred the whipped cream and caramel into his coffee.

"I got two more messages from the vet. She wants us to call her," Harper said.

"We've got to find the brother. He may be able to give us some insights into Bobbie. The vet may have to wait."

"So, I hear you've got a big game tonight. First night as a ref. Nervous?" Harper asked.

Lane thought for a moment. He remembered he still had to get new skates. "Arthur's buying me a referee's jersey and a pair of pants. But I've got to get a new helmet and skates."

"Have you ever skated without toe picks?" Harper smiled.

"No."

Harper smiled some more.

Harper continued smiling for the rest of the day until nearly four o'clock. It was a day of phone calls, faxes, and computer searches. As planned, they met in a conference room to compare notes.

Lane set several folders down on the table. Harper did the same. They sat next to one another with sleeves rolled up and jackets on the backs of their chairs.

Harper opened his top folder. "I've got a driver's license and photo of Jay Krocker. He's fifteen years younger than his sister. Owns a twenty-year-old Lincoln. I phoned the address on his driver's license. The woman who lives there said he drops by every month or so for mail. Apparently, he hasn't lived there for several years. Another place we might be able to find him is the university. He's registered there, and I've got a copy of his timetable. We should be able to wait around one of his classes, pick him out, and sit him down for a chat."

"And the report on his parents' house fire?" Lane asked.

"I did find some notes. The kid was barely fifteen at the time. He said his parents quit smoking. Bobbie had fought with them over money a couple of days before the fire. The firemen were able to save Jay because he was sleeping downstairs. But his parents died of smoke inhalation. According to the report, the batteries in both fire detectors were dead," Harper said.

"Who did the kid live with after the fire?"

"That's something we'll have to ask him," he said.

"We're short on physical evidence. Dr. Fibre has some physical evidence. Until we can supply him with evidence connecting individuals to crime scenes, he's not going to be able to help us much," Lane said.

"Aren't you gonna ask about the cops in Jamaica?"

"Well?" Lane asked.

"The officer I talked with has a cousin who works at the resort. There was a fight when Bobbie arrived for the second time. It was an argument between Bobbie and the twin sisters who died in the fire. Later, Bobbie was seen drinking with Frank—the GO—and the famous twins."

"The famous twins?" Lane asked.

"The twins had their own web site rating the sexual performances of the GO's at the various resorts," Harper said.

"GO's?" Lane leaned back in his chair.

"Don't you remember? Gigolos. Buff guys hired by resorts to entertain the guests. Apparently, the fabulous twins, Frank—the GO Bobbie fell for—and Bobbie drank into the wee hours. A few hours later, there was smoke coming out of the twins' room. Frank and the twins were found dead inside. Bobbie left on the plane later that day."

"Autopsy reports?" Lane asked.

Harper tapped a folder. "Faxed copies are in here. Frank and the twins died from smoke inhalation. All three had blood-alcohol levels of point-two-zero or higher. Both twins were smokers. The investigators attributed the cause of the fire to a cigarette left on the couch."

"A lot of careless smoking happens when Bobbie's around. Did your contact add anything else?" Lane asked.

"Just that the resort wants it all hushed up. It's bad for business when the tourists die. There were lots of rumours circulating the day after the fire. Bobbie packed up and left in the morning even though her flight didn't leave till seven o'clock."

"We need to talk with Bobbie's brother," Lane said.

+ + +

BOBBIE: Good afternoon. It's Bobbie on the ride home. I need your advice. How do I survive a life-threatening illness? It seems like when it rains, it pours. What do I do when my doctor tells me I've got cancer? It's Bobbie. Tell me your story and give me your advice.

+ + +

The arena smelled of sweat, propane fumes, and artificial ice. Arthur was waiting in the foyer and handed Lane a black bag. Arthur said, "Your new jersey, elbow pads, whistle, and pants are in there. You have to get your own helmet and skates." Arthur looked nervous as he eyed the door leading to the stands.

Lane said, "Thanks. Is Matt here?"

"He's getting changed." Arthur was sweating in spite of the chill in the air. "Never was very comfortable in places like this."

"Guess I'd better get changed." Lane walked down a hallway and knocked on a door labelled REFEREE.

"You need a key."

Lane turned. He was greeted by a fifty-something woman in a red and black flannel shirt, stretchy blue jeans, and running shoes. She looked like a gravel-truck driver and had the brushcut to prove it. "I'll open up for you today, but next time check in the office to pick up a key. Name's Cheryl." She stuck out a hand.

"Thanks." Lane shook her hand. Cheryl nearly broke his fingers with her grip.

She opened the door with a key on the end of a chain tied to her belt. "I'm the rink attendant. Gotta run. Game's almost over, and the ice needs a fresh coat."

Lane was lacing up his skates in the changing room, when a key turned in the lock.

"Hello," Lane said.

Bob, the head referee who'd taken an early dislike to Lane during the training sessions, walked in. "How'd you get in here?" he asked in his best drill-sergeant voice. "Cheryl the dyke let you in? Still got the figure skates I see."

Lane felt the heat rise on his face. He thought, *Just take a deep breath and ignore the jerk.*

"For the first few games the experienced refs come around and help the new guys out." Bob put his black equipment bag down. "You'll do the lines. I'll wear the red." He pulled out his jersey and pointed at the red band stitched around one arm.

Lane said nothing, did up his skates, and went outside. He held his whistle and Harper's ancient helmet in his right hand. Cheryl maneuvered the Zamboni off the ice, jumped down to scoop up a line of slush, then closed the gates behind her. The ice was blue-perfect. Lane felt a thrill of anticipation as he opened the gate and stepped down. His blades bit into the ice while he accelerated and put on his helmet.

Halfway into the game, Lane began to feel as if he were into a rhythm. He covered offsides at the blueline, fetched iced pucks for Bob, and thought only about the game. He was energized with a clear mind and the old, familiar feel of the ice underneath his blades. Looking the wrong way on a breakout play, Lane was blind-sided by two fifteen-year-old giants who collided, and slid into his knees. He found himself flat on his back with the wind knocked out of him, staring at the lights hanging from the arena ceiling. As awareness of his surroundings gradually returned, the two players got up and said, "Sorry Ref."

Lane blinked. He did a mental inventory of bones and muscles.

Bob bent over him and said, "Gotta keep your eyes open, buddy." He skated away without offering Lane a hand up.

On the next play, both of Matt's defencemen fell as they shifted from skating forward to skating in reverse. The opposing forward skated in on a breakaway.

Matt pushed himself out to the top of the crease. One shoulder was hunched higher than the other. His elbows were cocked too high.

Bob skated down the opposite side, getting into position to call the play.

The forward deked left.

Matt stood still.

The forward shot high on Matt's stick side.

His stick and blocker jerked up. There was nothing smooth about the motion. It appeared to be a hopeful swipe in the air in the vicinity of the puck. The puck bounced off Matt's blocker, over the glass, and through a gap in the net.

Bob blew the whistle.

Lane skated to the timekeeper for another puck. He returned to the face-off circle. Both centres were already in position.

Lane stopped and dropped the puck into Bob's waiting hand.

Bob smiled, "A cripple in net. Now I've seen everything!"

Even as Lane reacted, part of his mind told him not to. His right hand gripped the front of Bob's jersey. Lane's right skate hooked around and behind Bob's right ankle.

Both of Bob's hands gripped Lane's wrists. The veteran referee was pushed off balance and backward. Lane leaned forward, and knelt with a white-knuckled grip on Bob's jersey. Lane stopped Bob's head when it was a few centimetres from the ice.

Bob's eyes were wide open. Lane knelt close to Bob's ear and said, "That cripple is my nephew. Lay off!" Then, Lane lifted Bob up till he was momentarily vertical, with his skates off the ice, before setting him back on his feet. The entire incident happened so fast that nearly everyone who witnessed it assumed Lane had saved a falling Bob from hitting his head on the ice.

Matt's centre skated over to the goalie, said something only Matt could hear, and skated back for the face-off.

The game ended in a scoreless tie despite the fact that Matt's teammates ran out of steam with ten minutes remaining. Matt made one save after another, always having some part of his body in the way when the puck looked like it must go in the net. There was nothing graceful about his style. There was, however, an uncoordinated determination in the way he positioned himself to face skaters and the puck.

Two surprises awaited Lane when he left the ice.

"Hey, Ref!" Matt's coach called Lane over and offered his hand. "I'm Larry." He had a head carpeted with grey curly hair, evidence of the aftermath of teenaged acne on his face, and a pair of hearing aids. "Would you consider teaching the guys how to skate? It's gonna be a long season if they don't learn."

The second came after both referees changed in the locker room. Bob broke the silence, "Sorry man, what I said was outta line."

Too shocked to reply, Lane simply shook the hand Bob offered.

Inside the Jeep, on the way home, Arthur drove with his window rolled down, and the heater on high. "You two stink."

Matt turned in the front passenger seat to face Lane who sat in the back. Matt said, "Chad told me about what you said to the other ref. Thanks."

Arthur asked, "What did he say?"

Matt said, "The Ref called me a cripple. Uncle Lane shoved him to the ice and told him not to do that again."

Arthur said, "You what? Everybody in the stands thought the guy fell and you saved him."

Matt smiled. "I had a better angle."

+ + +

For a change, Tony drove the Lincoln on the way home from work. It was close to eleven o'clock.

"Man, I'm tired," Jay said.

"So, I've got it all figured out for Friday," Tony said.

Jay opened his eyes. They passed the Stampede Grounds. "This is the last time, right?"

"Sure. But it has to be good and this plan is great." Tony smiled while glancing sideways at Jay.

"But we need a third person this time."

"What do you mean?" Tony asked.

"Somebody to keep the stairs clear," Jay said.

"Who'd you have in mind?"

"Rosie."

Tony shook his head, "No way."

"It won't work then. Somebody's always going up or down those stairs."

"Uncle Tran wants to talk about you getting your own place."

"I've got a place to live. And don't change the subject." Jay sat up straight and adjusted the seat belt.

"A car, even a boat like this, isn't a place to live. Havin' your own place goes with being part of the family. You get a place to live and tuition is paid for. Uncle Tran's rules."

"What if I say no?" Jay asked.

Tony laughed. "We both know you're not gonna do that."

Jay shook his head and smiled.

"Now, have you got the masks?" Tony asked.

"In the trunk," Jay said.

"Good. We just need one more thing and we're ready."

Tuesday, October 20

Chapter 13

"WE'RE BEGINNING TO look like a cliché," Lane said. They sat at the window of the coffee shop on Kensington. Lane sipped a mocha. Harper drank his house roast.

"You should know better than to use big words around an uncultured cop like myself. Speaking of uncultured, Arthur told me about your little tussle last night. Not very suave, I must say." Harper sipped from his cup, leaving his pinky extended like a British flagpole.

"Do you ever get off the phone?" Lane asked.

"You know me, I keep one ear to the ground and one ear to my cellphone. So, don't change the subject. What happened?"

"The other Ref called Matt a cripple," Lane said.

"So, you flattened him?" Harper smiled.

"Sort of."

"And what did this Ref say after the game?"

"He apologized," Lane said.

"By the sound of things, Matt thinks you're some kind of saint."

"Apparently," Lane said.

"Enjoy it while you can. Those pedestals get to be pretty tippy. Still, I can see the kid continuing to grow on you. I've never seen you lose your cool. Maybe I'll go to the next game in case it happens again."

"Not likely," Lane said.

"It's funny how we'll take the nastiest comments about ourselves and not react, but when somebody says it to someone we care about, we go postal."

"So?" Lane decided to change the subject. "Hear from the chief?"

"As a matter of fact, after Bobbie's show yesterday afternoon, there were at least a hundred callers wondering why the Reddie case has not been closed."

"Did she mention it on her show?" Lane asked.

"Not a word. All she had to do was mention cancer, and people all over the city rushed to her rescue."

Lane's cell rang. He flipped it open. "Hello."

"Mr. Lane?" The woman's drawl came from somewhere south of there.

"Yes," Lane said.

"You're wondering how I got your cell number?"

"Yes, as a matter of fact," Lane said.

"Let's just say one of my clients has access. I'm Dr. Ellen Dent, veterinarian. I've been trying to reach you for almost a week now."

"We're happy with Riley's vet." Lane made ready to press the end button.

"I've never been in a position where it became necessary to solicit patients. This call is about another animal altogether." The way Dent said 'animal' piqued Lane's interest.

"And?" Lane felt a bit perplexed by Dr. Ellen Dent, her accent, and her condescension.

"I believe a certain 'animal' and I might have

something to offer you in the way of information about the Reddie murders."

Lane's entire mind focused on the conversation. He remembered Lisa's comment about the canine hairs on Kaylie's clothing. "Go on."

"We need to meet. I have evidence, and you need to see it to understand," Dr. Dent said.

"When?"

"I have an opening in thirty minutes."

"Where are you?" Lane asked.

"Crowfoot Animal Rescue Emergency. That's CARE for short," Dr. Dent said.

"We'll be there." Lane thought, *This one sounds like she's crazy.*

On the way to CARE, they drove by the sign at Bobbie's church. There was a new message: *Even in the darkest of times, God shines her light on me.*

"We're five minutes late," Lane said as they parked. The sign outside the office had CARE in metre-high blue letters on a white background. Inside, a grey cat sat on a chair. It held out a paw to reveal blue nail polish.

"Hello. He likes to show off his nails after we paint them." The receptionist smiled, revealing braces. "You must be Mr. Lane."

"That's right," Lane said.

"Dr. Ellen Dent is waiting," the receptionist said in a tone that warned the doctor did not like being behind schedule. "This way." She led them to the examination room at the end of a hall stacked with bags of dog food. "She'll be right with you."

Lane and Harper stood inside a small examination room next to a belt-high Arborite table. Behind the table were enough diplomas to cover a living room wall. Lane wondered if all three examination rooms were wallpapered the same way.

"What is it with this Dr. Ellen Dent thing? Who is she trying to impress?" Harper asked.

Lane shrugged. The back door opened, and the doctor arrived. Her grey hair was cut short. She wore an immaculate white smock. Dr. Dent had a chart tucked under one elbow. In the other hand, she carried a small, grey, wire-haired dog of mixed parentage. One of the dog's ears was bandaged, and its front right paw was in a cast. The dog's tail wagged.

"I'm Dr. Ellen Dent," the vet said. She gently set the dog on the examination table and kept her left hand close to protect it. She put on black-framed reading glasses and balanced the open chart in her right hand.

Harper and Lane looked at one another and prepared to be lectured.

Harper said, "Detective Cameron Mitchell Richard Harper at your service, Ma'am. This is Lane."

Lane watched Harper's face for a hint of a snicker.

"We don't have a great deal of time, so I'll get right to the point," Dr. Dent said, apparently impervious to Harper's sarcasm. "This dog's name is Eddie. I'm trained to observe the dog and its people. This dog is only two years old, and it has been here often. The morning the Reddie child disappeared, we found it at the back door in a cardboard box." The vet pointed at the dog's injured leg. "It's reasonable to assume the dog's paw was struck with a hammer." Dr. Dent then lifted the dog's chin. "This ear was removed. Dogs sometimes have their ears tattooed or a microchip inserted. Remove either and remove any chance at positive identification."

"You said you had information about the Reddie murders," Harper said.

"Bobbie Reddie brought Eddie in on six separate occasions. In each case, the children were with her. Each of Eddie's legs was broken once. Ribs were broken on either side of the rib cage. I know this dog is Eddie, but I can't prove it. Ms. Reddie always insisted I give her the negatives when we took X-rays. I believe that Bobbie abused the dog to control the children," Dr. Dent said.

"What makes you think she's responsible?" Harper asked.

"The way Eddie shied from Ms. Reddie, and the way the dog tried to stay close to the boy," Dr. Dent said.

Lane noticed the woman was beginning to shake. "But how can you be certain of this?"

"You have to understand." Dr. Dent's voice began to break. "My father did it to me. I know what she did to this animal. I know it in a way I can't explain." She began to sob. Eddie licked her hand. "Someone has to protect that child. This Bobbie, I know what she is." Dr. Dent's eyes were dripping tears, and her nose started to run. She had no free hand, so she bent to wipe her nose on the back of her sleeve. "You musn't think I'm a crazy person. I know that the child is in danger. I don't know what the law allows you to do, but . . ."

Lane took the file from her and handed her a tissue. "Could we start with a hair and blood sample from Eddie? We may be able to do a DNA match. It's a place for us to begin."

"Of course." Dr. Dent wiped her nose. "I'll do it right away."

Harper asked, "What time was the dog found?"

"When Helen arrived at 7:00 AM," Dr. Dent said.

"How attached was the boy to the dog?" Lane asked.

"Eddie tucked himself close to Cole and never took his eyes off of Ms. Reddie."

+ + +

Harper drove as they headed back to the centre of town.

"What the hell was that all about?" Harper asked. "I mean one minute she's very definitely in control and the next she's in tears."

Lane thought while he read the other side of the sign next to Bobbie's church. This side read: *Out of the depths I cry out to you O Lord.*

Lane said, "We'll have to wait for the results of the DNA tests. If Dent's right, then the dog hairs on Kaylie's clothing will match Eddie's."

"The problem is, none of this stuff is the kind of evidence we need to make a conviction. We'd get laughed out of court with the Jamaica resort story, Eddie's DNA, and the shredded car. The defense would say we've been reading too many tabloids, and they'd be right."

"Still, we have to see the patterns developing here. Three separate incidents where careless smoking was linked to fatalities. A new car is destroyed and any potential evidence is conveniently destroyed right along with it. On top of this, there is mounting pressure to close the case and clear Bobbie. It's when you look at all that we've got that this case begins to become clear."

"I'm not so sure. It's like Bobbie's been your prime suspect from the first time you met her," Harper said.

Lane said, "You're right. But that doesn't make me wrong. If we hurry, we might catch Bobbie's brother at the university."

In fifteen minutes, they drove past the university's arts parkade, where Jay's Lincoln was parked, and pulled up at the meters in front of the education building. "His class is in the there. First floor," Harper pointed at the brick building. He turned of the engine and palmed the keys.

Lane stepped out of the Chevy.

The sun was warm on their backs, but the wind's cool breath promised that winter was on its way. They pulled open the doors of the education building and stepped inside. On the left was a coffee shop, chairs, and tables. On the right was the room they were looking for. Lane pulled a copy of Jay's photo ID out of his pocket and studied it. "Need to take a look?" He handed it to Harper.

They pulled on the door and walked inside the lecture theatre.

+ + +

Jay always sat at the front, so the tape recorder could pick up the professor's voice. He looked over his shoulder at the clock and saw the pair of detectives. When he was a kid, he had learned to spot them. After his parents died in the fire, there were police all over the front yard. He had made up a game of guessing which ones were the police, which ones were the reporters, and who the spectators were. It had been a way to keep his mind off what happened to his parents. Between sobs he'd tried to explain what he knew about Bobbie, but the police had ignored him and listened only to his sister.

These detectives stood just inside the door. The one with the moustache was younger and looked like a football player. The older one was about the same height, had thinning hair, and it looked like he was missing part of his ear. He didn't look like a cop. There was something different about him, Jay decided.

Jay shuddered when he remembered the accident on Crowchild Trail. He thought about the Toyota pickup. He saw it veer off the pavement and up onto its side in a cloud of dust and debris.

Jay turned around, reached into his backpack and lifted out a toque. He pulled it on.

+ + +

Lane scanned the crowd. The class was filling up.

Harper said, "Excuse me. We're police officers looking for Jay Krocker." He showed the driver's license photo of Jay to a man of about forty-five with an athletic build and a ready smile.

The professor was caught off balance, "I've got eighty-five students in this class. He doesn't look familiar."

Lane thought for a minute, then said, "Would you ask if he's here?"

The professor went down the stairs and stood at the front of the class. "Is there a Jay Krocker here today?" He looked past Jay and up at the officers as students looked at one another and shrugged. "Sorry," the professor said, a little too quickly.

Harper held up his right hand as if to say thank you.

Lane began to walk down the stairs. Students looked up at him. He studied their faces.

"Is that all you need? I would like to get this class started," the professor said.

Lane spotted a student wearing a toque. The student stood up and made for the door to his left. The door closed behind him.

Lane followed and opened the door. He looked right and left down the empty hallway.

Harper came around the corner to Lane's left. Lane ran to his right and reached the end of the hallway. The door to his left led outside. A clutch of students came through the door. Lane looked right. The hallway was empty.

"Well?" Harper pulled up next to Lane.

"All we've done is scare him off," Lane said.

"Today's not a total loss. I mean, we've got the dog's blood and hair sample. Maybe we'll get a match with Kaylie's clothing," Harper said.

+ + +

"Jay, over here!"

Jay almost had a heart attack. He turned and saw Rosie. Black leather jacket, blue pants and cowboy boots. He thought, *How is it possible for one person to look so good?* Jay looked around to see if the police officers were nearby.

"Come on, we can talk and walk." Rosie adjusted the nylon book bag hanging from a strap on her shoulder. "I always carry too many books on Tuesday."

"Want me to carry them for you?" Jay asked.

"I was just complaining, not asking for help," Rosie said.

He had to pick up his pace to keep up with her. They moved north toward the library. "How'd you find me?"

"Tony," she said as if the answer was obvious. "He says he always knows where to find you because you're so predictable. And he says you want help on Friday night."

"Yes. We need help or it won't work."

"This is for my cousin, right?" She stopped to study his face.

"The one with the baby?" Jay asked.

"You guys pulled off the last one at the hockey game?"

"Uh, yeah." Jay made a mental note to tell Tony to keep his big mouth shut.

"There's a picture in the *The Gauntlet* today. Rex has that thing around his neck, and the newspaper caption says, "Rex is a dickhead." My cousin will like that. Rosie smiled.

Jay unzipped his jacket. He felt warm in spite of the north wind. "Good."

"I've got ten friends who want to help. We'll be there Friday night right after the first game. You be ready."

"But—" Jay said.

"Don't worry. We know what to do. You two just have to do your part. See you then." Rosie turned left into the library.

+ + +

BOBBIE: Good afternoon. It's Bobbie on the ride home. Thank you for the overwhelming support. I need more advice about a related topic. When you've got a terminal illness, what do you tell your child? I, and many women like me, could sure use some advice. I'm Bobbie, speak to me.

+ + +

Jay and Tony sat together in the mall, sipping coffee, and watching the people. They had twenty-three minutes before their shift started at 8:30 PM.

"How come you told Rosie about the plan?" Jay asked.

"You said we needed help. I asked her, she said no."

Tony leaned back. People had to take a detour, or trip over his outstretched feet.

"Well, she said yes this afternoon. She asked if we were the ones who got Rex at the hockey game. Did you see the picture in the paper?" Jay asked.

"A classic. That and the caption. Man, who says revenge isn't sweet?" Tony closed his eyes as if trying to hold onto the image in his mind.

"The cops are looking for me," Jay said.

Tony sat up, "What?"

"They came to my psych class. They told the prof to ask for me. I left class early."

Tony studied his coffee cup. "Why would they want you?"

"I cut this guy off on Crowchild Trail. He rolled his truck up on its side," Jay said.

"Did your car hit his truck?"

"No," Jay said.

"Did he die?"

"Don't think so," Jay said.

"Did you check the news or read the papers?" Tony asked.

"No!"

"Do you realize how crazy that sounds?" Tony asked.

"Not as crazy as you might think," Jay said.

Wednesday, October 21

Chapter 14

ARTHUR SMILED AND passed Lane the newspaper's city section. "Read this." He pointed at an article on page three.

Lane set his toast down and took the paper.

"You're going to love it," Arthur said when Lane began to read.

> **CITY WOMAN WINS RECOGNITION**
>
> The winner of the Daughters of Alberta (DOA) award for Outstanding Citizen of the Year is Mrs. Charity Smallway. Smallway is a twenty-year member of DOA.
>
> "Charity has been recognized for her service to the community," Mrs. Constance Dupuis, the chair of DOA explained at the Palliser Hotel awards ceremony.
>
> Mrs. Smallway has been a champion of family values and fundraiser for many local charity organizations. Mrs. Smallway said, "I'm thrilled to be honoured in this way by women with moral integrity."

Lane asked, "It's really called DOA? like 'Dead on arrival?'"

Arthur said, "Apparently. And just in case you forgot, Matt's game starts at eight tonight."

"Still haven't got those new skates," Lane said.

"Better hurry and get ready. Dr. Keeler said 7:30 AM."

Lane smiled as he stood up from the kitchen table. "This is a switch. Keeler's calling me for an appointment."

"No indication what it's about?" Arthur asked.

"None. He just said he wanted to talk with me, alone. I haven't had any tests lately, have I?"

"Not that I can think of. Are you going to tell him the nightmares are coming back?" Arthur asked.

Half an hour later Lane stood in the empty hallway outside Dr. Keeler's office door. Lane knocked. He heard the deadbolt turn, then he was facing Dr. Keeler. He still reminded Lane of a horror writer, with his black hair, lined face and dark eyes accented by thumb-sized eyebrows. Keeler stood a good head shorter than the detective.

"Thanks for coming." Keeler shook Lane's hand.

The doctor looked as if he hadn't slept last night.

"We can talk in my office." Keeler lead the way down the hall until they reached his office set in one corner of the building. He ushered Lane in and closed the door behind them. He sat down beside Lane.

"You've got me worried." Lane turned to look at the doctor.

"This is a very difficult situation." Keeler was looking sideways at Lane. "I've been worrying about this for almost a week, then things came to a head yesterday." He leaned forward.

Lane said, "I'm really in the dark here. What

exactly are we talking about?"

"Bobbie Reddie's radio show. She told her audience that she has cancer."

Lane leaned back and put his hand to his mouth. Forcing himself to wait so the doctor could get his story out.

"What I'm about to tell you is breaking doctor–patient confidentiality. Another doctor has confided her concerns to me. You see, Bobbie was tested for cancer, and the biopsy was negative."

Lane nodded and waited.

"You're promising me this will stay confidential?" Keeler asked.

"Yes."

"A child's safety is at stake. I'm getting ahead of myself. I should have had a cup of coffee this morning." Keeler shook his head to clear his mind. "Bobbie doesn't have cancer, yet she's acting as if she does. And she has been exhibiting signs of Munchausen's Syndrome by Proxy."

Lane held out his hands to signal his ignorance.

"She brought her children in to her family doctor with a wide variety of symptoms. My colleague tried to diagnose the symptoms but was always mystified until she considered Munchausen's. It appears that Bobbie Reddie was causing her children to become ill, then taking them to the doctor. This went on for more than a year. My friend confronted Bobbie, and Ms. Reddie promptly threatened the doctor with a malpractice suit. Then Reddie moved on to another doctor. I checked with the next doctor. She is also becoming suspicious. You see, I'm breaking an oath in telling you this, but I feel I have no choice because of the child. The surviving child is at tremendous risk."

"How did you know I was investigating the Reddie murders?" Lane asked.

"It was reasonable to assume you are the investigator. You always come to me asking about cases which start out with missing persons," Keeler said.

Lane smiled. "A good bit of deduction."

"My colleague and I believe that the boy is in danger. The children's symptoms were becoming more severe. It's one of the reasons why Ms. Reddie was confronted."

"Did you contact social services?" Lane asked.

"Munchausen's is very hard to prove. We really only arrived at the conclusion, because all other possibilities had been eliminated. We'd hoped Ms. Reddie would be willing to seek treatment," Keeler said.

"So, you were consulted by the other doctor on the Reddie case?" Lane asked.

"Yes."

"Did the father ever come on the visits?"

"Not once," Keeler said.

+ + +

BOBBIE: Good afternoon. It's Bobbie on the ride home. Today we have a special guest, Charity Smallway. She's this year's winner of the Daughters of Alberta Outstanding Citizen of the Year Award. Charity is here to talk about the exploitation of children.

How do we protect our children from those who would harm them?

+ + +

Jay picked up a piece of beef with his chopsticks. The chili peppers in the satay beef-noodle soup cleared his sinuses. It was his first meal of the day. He sat across the table from Tony who tackled a bowl of noodles and chicken. The Lucky Elephant Restaurant was about half full.

"Where's Uncle Tran?" Jay asked.

"I don't know. There's a hockey game tonight. He's addicted to it," Tony said.

"What's Rosie got planned for tomorrow night?" Jay asked.

"She says we'll know what to do. Whatever she has planned will happen after the first match." Tony wiped his mouth with a napkin.

"Match?" Jay inhaled a mouthful of rice noodles.

"It's volleyball. You know, the Hemi."

"Hemi?" Jay asked.

"Man, I always know more about what's goin' on in this town than you do. Teams from all over the western hemisphere come here every year to play volleyball. It's on network TV. Big sponsors, big names, big bucks. The place'll be packed."

"Oh," Jay said.

"You gotta start reading a paper or listening to the radio." Tony shook his head.

"Not gonna happen," Jay said.

+ + +

Lane circled the ice after setting the nets and making sure all of the gates were closed. The ice was perfect. *Cheryl's an artist,* he thought. In her hands, the Zamboni creates a perfectly smooth surface.

"Hey Ref! They're really scrapin' the bottom of the barrel when they take some fruit in figure skates!"

Lane glanced up into the stands.

A man in a full-length black leather coat, black leather driving gloves, and tie pointed at Lane. "That's right, you!" He laughed at Lane.

Lane looked away. *This is going to be lots of fun,* he thought. Matt lead his team out onto the ice. They wore new jerseys tonight; red, white, and black. Matt nearly fell. He turned, righted himself, circled, and stopped. The player behind him stopped by falling. The rest of the team managed ragged and juddering braking maneuvers. Lane looked at Matt's coach who smiled back. *He's right,* Lane thought, *these guys really do need some skating lessons.*

Lane was the only referee to show for the game and, as a result, heard only a fraction of what the heckler in black leather had to scream. It was another shutout for Matt who managed to stop the puck with toes, blocker, pads, elbows, and helmet. Somehow, he even stopped a puck with his backside turned to the play and one eye on the puck. *It was never pretty,* Lane thought, *but the kid got it done.*

It was about halfway through the game, just after Lane blew the whistle on an icing, when Matt skated to the centre line across from his team's bench. He looked up into the stands and struck the glass with his stick. "Shut up!"

Lane looked up into the stands. The man in black leather said, "It's a free country kid!"

Lane skated over to Matt. "What's the matter?"

Matt's face was red behind the mask. His eyes were animal. "Didn't you hear what he said?"

"No." Lane looked up at the man in black leather. Cheryl the rink attendant was coming down the aisle with a wet mop. She was followed by three other women who were mothers of players on Matt's team. None of the women were smiling.

"Gotta clean up the mess," Cheryl said.

"What mess?" black leather asked.

"You, Mac," one of the mothers said.

"Whatdoyamean?" Mac asked.

Another woman said, "We mean it's time for you to go, Mac. Our boys put up with you last year. It's not gonna happen again this year."

"I got a right to watch my kid play!" Mac said.

Cheryl slapped the mop onto the cement at Mac's feet.

"Hey, those shoes cost me three-hundred bucks!" Mac stood up and backed away. "I'm gonna have your job, dyke!" He raised a fist.

The third woman pulled out a cellphone, "I think that's called attempted assault. I'll check it out with the police."

"Go ahead. Guy can't have a little fun at a game

these days without havin' to put up with a politically correct gang of dykes!" Mac retreated.

The women waited till the arena door closed behind Mac.

Cheryl leaned on her mop and smiled at Matt. "Finish the game fellas, another team's up after you."

After the game, when Lane, Arthur, and Matt drove home, the Jeep filled with a now familiar pungent mixture of sweat and drying equipment.

Matt said, "Why do you take that? I mean the Ref calls me a cripple, and you've got him by the throat. The guy in the stands calls you a fudge-packer, and you do nothin.'"

Lane had his window cracked open to let in some fresh air.

"Didn't you hear what he said?" Matt asked.

"Some of it," Lane said.

Matt shook his head.

"After you accept who you are, people can't say much to hurt you," Arthur said.

Lane thought, *It's time to change the subject.* "Why don't we get Martha to come to the next game?"

Friday, October 23

Chapter 15

LANE WAS AT least fifteen minutes ahead of the morning rush hour traffic when his cellphone rang. He reached into his pocket, flipped the phone open, and pressed the talk button.

"Lane?" Lisa said.

"Good morning."

"I phoned Arthur but you had already left," Lisa said.

"What's up?" Lane thought, *Don't forget to ask her about Loraine.*

"Some more information's been passed on to me. Dr. Fibre couldn't find any matches from the scene except those from the cushion Kaylie was lying on," Lisa said.

"Do you mean that Kaylie was placed in the camper and not moved?" Lane watched the traffic ahead of him and checked his rear-view mirrors. He was all alone for the moment.

"Looks like. And there's more. Kaylie died from Shaken Baby Syndrome. Beyond that, there is evidence of past childhood injuries. The coroner is checking with the family doctor to see if there might be a history of abuse."

"That is supported by another source," Lane said.

"Are you holding out on me?" Lisa asked.

"A little," Lane said.

"The physical evidence is saying two very distinct things. Kaylie died before her father, and her body was transported to the crime scene," Lisa said.

"I've got some canine samples waiting at the lab to determine if we've got a match for the dog hairs found on her clothes."

"That would be a good start, but we'll need more," Lisa said.

Lane said, "And there's something else. Does Loraine have any experience working with kids who survive this kind of trauma?"

"I'll ask her. I've hardly seen her the last few days, it's been so busy. I'll get back to you." Lisa hung up.

Five minutes later, Lane was driving east along Memorial Drive. A light fog hung over the river. The lights near the Louise Bridge turned red, and the phone rang.

"Lane," he said while stopping short of the crosswalk.

"It's me," Harper said. "Still haven't found this Jay character. Put out some flags. So if he shows up on our doorstep, we should hear about it. May have a line on his employer, though. How about you?"

"Lisa just called. Looks like Kaylie died elsewhere and was transported to the campsite. I keep remembering how clean the soles of her running shoes were. Anyway, she died before her father, but we figured that anyway," Lane said. The light turned green, and he was able to turn right over the bridge. "I'll be there in ten or fifteen minutes."

"You can tell me all about the hockey game," Harper said.

"You're too well informed for my own good."

+ + +

BOBBIE: Good afternoon. It's Bobbie on the ride home. They say God never hands me more than I can handle. I want to wrap up the week with your stories of surviving the tragedies in our lives. It's Bobbie, speak to me.

+ + +

"Where are they?" Tony asked. Jay and Tony stood, leaning on the round metal railing, looking down at the volleyball match. The floor of the gymnasium was two storeys below them. It looked like this game might end at any moment.

"This is huge," Jay said. The fans in the stands sat in rows of red plastic chairs descending to the court below. Not one of the seats was empty. The crowd went silent when the server leapt and arched his back to pound the ball over the net.

"This is a big deal. That's the point. We can make Rex look like a fool in front of thousands of fans," Tony said.

The opposition bumped the ball back over to the Dinos' side of the court. One of the Dino players spiked the ball onto the floor. The ball bounced up into the stands. The crowd roared. The referee raised an index finger and pointed at the Dinos. "One more point, and this one's over," Tony said.

Jay looked around the court, "There are cameras everywhere."

"When we put our masks on, we look like presidents. No one will know it's us. Don't worry," Tony smiled. "The toboggan is over there behind the pillar. We'll change as soon as—"

"Here they come," Jay said.

Rex followed a young woman wearing a pale yellow dress reaching from her throat to her ankles. As she moved, the dress flowed behind. She held one of Rex's hands. Jay was pretty sure the mascot was drooling.

"Hurry!" Tony moved back away from the railing. They ducked behind the pillar. Presidential masks were pulled out of a backpack. Tear-away sweatpants and shirts were stuffed into the pack. Jay reached behind the pillar and pulled out a two-metre wooden toboggan they'd stashed earlier in the day. They moved in behind Rex.

Up ahead, a procession of young women turned heads as they crossed the open area on the upper level of the gymnasium. They moved toward the stairway leading down to the volleyball court. The women were dressed like the one wearing pale yellow. They were, however, wearing shades of orange and purple. Rosie was in the lead, wearing red. All of the women wore their black hair in single braids reaching down to the gentle curves at the small of their backs.

A whistle blew. The crowd roared. "Dinos win!" the announcer said.

Rosie led the women to the top of the stairs then stepped down.

Jay and Tony trailed an oblivious Rex.

One by one, people turned to watch the procession of young women until everyone had their eyes on the ten who moved with uniform precision. Each step was preceded by a pause. The women appeared to move as one person. Jay had to force himself to take his eyes away from Rosie.

The crowd became completely silent.

Even the announcer was quiet as the women in the flowing dresses swept down toward the court.

Jay thought, *Everyone thinks this is part of the show.*

At court level, Rosie pushed triangular barriers aside and stepped out. Players, who'd gone to their benches, turned to watch. All around the court, cameras focussed on the procession.

The ten women broke into two groups of five facing one other. In one graceful motion, they raised their arms to point up the stairway to Rex who stood at the top.

The woman in yellow stepped away from Rex.

Tony and Jay grabbed either side of the toboggan and hit Rex behind the knees with the toboggan's round-wooden nose. Rex fell backward onto the wood. Tony and Jay aimed Rex, then shoved him forward, and down the stairs.

"SHIT!" Rex's toboggan skipped and clattered, gathering speed as it rushed to court level.

The crowd's laughter started somewhere to Jay's left and grew until it deafened him.

The toboggan carried Rex right to the bottom of the steps and slithered sideways across the polished wooden floor. The deceleration—when the toboggan hit the court—was terrific. Rex rolled sideways and ended up at Rosie's feet. Jay watched as Rosie bent down to say something to Rex.

"Bitch!" Rex said.

It was as if this was the signal for the procession to scatter. The young women raced for exits on either side of the court.

"Let's go!" Tony ran for the change room where they'd stashed spare clothing.

Jay looked down.

Rex had grabbed hold of Rosie's arm and raised his fist.

Jay stopped, backtracked and, before he could think to run away, headed for the stairs. He rushed down, taking the steps two at a time.

Rex struck Rosie across the face.

"Hey!" a woman in the crowd said.

The rest of the crowd remained silent.

Jay's knees buckled when he jumped off the last step and hit the court. He rolled. Back up on his feet, he headed for Rex. The mascot raised his fist to strike for a third time. Jay jumped, grabbed the raised arm, and pulled Rex sideways. Rosie fell free.

Rosie grabbed Jay's arm to help him up. They ran along behind the the stands, into the hallway, and toward the skating oval. She pulled up her dress and ran next to him. Jay saw that she was wearing running shoes. He was having trouble keeping up with her. They shoved open a pair of metal doors. An underground hallway took a blind turn to the right.

Rosie looked back over her shoulder. "Hurry! Security's after us!"

"No sense being in a rush now," a woman's voice said. Two police officers turned the corner and faced the fugitives.

"Shit!" Rosie skidded, stopped, regained her balance, and found she'd stuck her nose between the breasts of one police officer.

"We'd like a word with the pair of you," the male officer said.

Jay looked at Rosie. Rosie backed away from the female officer.

Rosie smiled. "Not a problem, officers."

The male officer spoke into his radio, "Got them."

+ + +

"Lane? It's Harper. We've got a line on Jay Krocker. It has to be now."

Lane looked across the dinner table at Arthur and Matt. He sighed and spoke into the phone. "Where?"

+ + +

Jay was in the room next to Rosie's. They were in a couple of offices just beyond the courtyard next to the fitness centre. The female officer took her time getting

Jay's name and other particulars. She even managed to hunt him down a Hemi T-shirt to cover his naked torso. He was sitting alone at a round table, when two men stepped in. Right away, he recognized them as the two cops who had come to his psychology class.

"I'm Harper and this is Lane," the larger of the two said.

Jay watched Lane, who was dressed in a shirt and sports jacket. Lane's eyes were sizing him up. It seemed to Jay that Lane was more curious than anything else.

"We're here to ask you some questions," Lane said.

"What am I being charged with?" Jay was certain he was about to be kicked out of university. *There goes the scholarship,* he thought.

"We're not here to charge you with anything." Lane sat down next to Jay. The wheels on his chair squeaked. "We're here on an entirely separate matter."

Harper sat down on the other side of the table, effectively eliminating any hope of Jay's escaping.

Man, here it comes, Jay thought. *They're gonna ask about the Toyota pickup.*

"Are you related to Bobbie Reddie?" Lane asked.

Jay sat back. He thought, *Of all the questions they could have asked, of all the questions I prepared for, not this one.* "She's my sister."

"When was the last time you saw her?" Harper asked.

"My niece's birthday party," Jay said.

"Your niece's name?" Lane asked.

"Kaylie," Jay said.

"When was this birthday party?" Harper asked.

"May."

"Does Cole have a dog?" Lane asked.

"Eddie," Jay said.

"You're sure the dog's name is Eddie?" Harper pulled out a folding keyboard with a tiny screen. When it was assembled, Harper began to type.

"Yep," Jay said, finally.

Lane looked at Harper who typed and nodded once.

"Are you aware that Kaylie and Charles Reddie are dead?" Lane asked.

"What?" Jay felt numb. "What did you say?"

"Kaylie and Charles are dead," Harper said.

"No way!" Jay sat back, then leaned forward. His chin touched his chest. *Not again,* he thought. *This can't be happening, again.*

Lane said, "Their bodies were found in a camper. Were you not contacted about the funeral?"

"I live in my car," Jay said without thinking. "I don't have a phone, don't watch the news, don't listen to the radio." He looked up. "Is Cole dead too?"

"No. Cole is alive," Harper said.

"Was there a fire?" Jay asked.

"Fire?" Lane concentrated on Jay's reaction.

"You heard me. Was there a fire?" Jay asked.

Lane studied Jay. So far, Jay was telling the truth. He watched the young man in the black T-shirt put his head on his palm. Jay's hair was a tangled mess from the mask he'd been wearing. Lane tried to remember all he had been told outside the room. The officers had briefed them on the prank the Presidential Brothers and Rosie had pulled off earlier in the evening. Apparently, the young woman down the hall had decided to charm all who came in contact with her. Rex, on the other hand had offended nearly everyone. No one was impressed by the marks he had left on Rosie's face.

"There was a burned-out cigarette butt. It didn't ignite the cushion's fabric," Lane said.

Jay sat and scratched his head. It sounded like he was going to break the skin. "Cole's a smart kid. He's too bright for his own good."

"What are you saying?" Lane asked.

"If Cole's still alive, he's a witness. He knows what happened. He's a threat," Jay said.

"A threat?" Lane asked.

"To my sister! Jesus, are you listening? The first chance she gets, she'll get rid of the threat!" Jay glared at Lane.

"Explain," Lane said.

"When I was fifteen, my sister was in debt. She'd gambled away whatever she could get her hands on. She and Charles were gonna lose their house. Bobbie came to my parents and demanded money. For the first time in their lives, they said no. The next night, the house burned down. My parents died. I was put in the hospital. My sister came to visit me. She brought Cole. You know what she said to me?"

Lane waited.

Harper looked up.

Jay closed his eyes. "'I'm so afraid Cole will die in his sleep.' That's what she said to me. It's how my sister makes threats. 'I'm so afraid you'll fall down the stairs' is what she said before she pushed me down the basement steps, when I was eight. When she said she was afraid Cole would die in his sleep, it was a warning. If I didn't keep my mouth shut, Cole would die."

"So, what did you do?" Lane asked.

"I disappeared so she couldn't trace me. Lived with different friends. Got a job. Bought a car and lived in it. Nearly froze to death a couple of times the first winter. Made sure I never missed the kids' birthdays. That way my sister would know I was still around. I thought that way it might mean the kids would be safe. Shit! I was so stupid."

"What happens now that Bobbie's broken the agreement?" Lane asked.

"No one's gonna believe me. I mean my sister is Bobbie Reddie. She's on the radio. She goes to church. Some people think she's a saint. She can make anyone believe anything she wants. Who would believe what a homeless jerk like me has to say?" Jay asked.

There was a knock at the door.

"Come in," Harper said.

The door opened. The female officer said, "Tommy Pham is here. Says he's Jay's lawyer."

+ + +

"We were mining gold until the lawyer showed up," Harper said after Jay left.

"Still we have a lot more than we had before we talked with him." Lane put his hands behind his head, leaned back, and stretched.

"You know, we had him for less than an hour and a lawyer shows up. That's pretty fast," Harper said. "Especially since Jay was more surprised than we were when the lawyer arrived."

"I was thinking the same thing. Can we find out who the lawyer works for?" Lane asked.

Saturday, October 24

Chapter 16

ARTHUR HUNG UP the phone. He looked at Lane. "Martha's being released from the hospital."

"When?" Lane had the TV on. Paired figure skaters swept from the left of the screen to the right.

"Turn it off. You haven't been watching anyway. You're too into this damned case," Arthur said.

Lane reached for the remote. The screen went blank.

"The test results came in. The cancer has spread. Martha starts chemo on Monday. They gave her the option of being an outpatient, and she took it." Arthur sat across from Lane.

"We have to tell Matt," Lane said.

"I know." Arthur began to weep.

Sunday, October 25

Chapter 17

JAY STOOD BAREFOOTED on the concrete of the parkade. He wore sweatpants and a T-shirt. Steam rose from a puddle of his urine. He tucked himself in. *I've been in my car for two days,* he thought. The twilight stretched shadows. He looked over at the open back door of his Lincoln. Jay moved toward it, climbed in, and slid his feet into his sleeping bag to warm them. He reached up to pull the door closed.

He tugged.

The door stuck.

"You really know how to make an impression. I mean that picture of you taking a pee up against the parkade wall will stay with me forever."

Jay looked back over his shoulder.

Rosie looked down at him. "It doesn't smell pretty in there."

"How'd you find me?" Jay sat up. *My breath must smell horrible,* he thought.

"I've been searching all day. Tony said you lived in your car, so we started checking all the university parking lots. This was second from the last on my list," Rosie said.

"Where's Tony?" Jay asked.

"His Mom grounded him for the weekend. My dad wanted to do the same, but I talked him out of it."

There was a question in Jay's glance.

"He told me to come and look for you." Rosie looked at him. The swelling on her cheek had shrunk. It blended green, yellow, and purple. "What happened when the police interrogated you?"

Jay shook his head. He took a long breath. "They told me my niece is dead."

"What?"

"Kaylie and her father, Charles, are dead. Kaylie is my sister's kid. She just had a birthday. She was full of attitude and had just learned to ride her bike. She was so proud she could ride a two-wheeler. That kid was so coordinated."

Rosie stood still, speechless.

"They said it looked like a murder suicide. No way. Charles was kind, gentle, and really naive. My sister did it. Just like she killed my parents," Jay said.

"What are you talkin' about?" Rosie wrapped her arms around her shoulders.

"When I was fifteen, my house burned, and my parents died. My sister started the fire."

"She's out of jail?" Rosie asked.

"My sister never went to jail. Instead, she inherited half of my parents' estate," Jay said.

"What?" Rosie asked.

"My sister is Bobbie Reddie. You know, Bobbie on the radio."

"'Speak to me' Bobbie?"

"That's right," Jay said.

Rosie looked over the roof of the car.

"That's how it works. As soon as I mention her

name, people have their doubts. They think Bobbie is some kind of saint. You might have believed all of what I just told you, up to the point where I mentioned her name."

Rosie looked at him again. "You came back for me. Everyone else ran, and you came back for me. All my friends, even some of my relatives, left me there. The police would never have caught you, if you hadn't come back for me."

Jay leaned his head to the left and wondered what was coming next. *Usually, I'm the one running away,* he thought. "What are you saying?"

"I'm saying . . ." she began, then thought for a moment. "You figure it out."

"I hope someone will help Cole when he figures it out," Jay said.

"Cole? Who's he?" Rosie sounded exasperated with the ever-expanding list of complications in Jay's life.

"My nephew. If anyone knows what really happened to Kaylie and Charles, Cole does," Jay said.

Rosie watched Jay.

"It's only a matter of time before he disappears. He's smart. He figures things out. The kid was reading at four. People think because he doesn't say much, there's not much going on in his head. They're wrong. Cole used to talk with me. He'll know what Bobbie did. And she'll know it too. Cole will have to be dealt with before he says something to the wrong person."

"Come on. Get behind the wheel. Follow me," Rosie said.

"Why?" Jay asked.

"Uncle Tran has got you an apartment. It's definitely a step up from this place." Rosie looked inside Jay's car. "It's even partially furnished. And, it has a bathroom. You could use some cleaning up, cracker." She laughed and walked toward her car.

Monday, October 26

Chapter 18

"I'LL PICK UP Matt at school after she calls," Arthur said.

"The room ready?" Lane dug into a grapefruit.

"It's all ready." Arthur stood up from the kitchen table then sat back down again. "I'm worried."

"About your sister?" Lane went to pick up his glass of orange juice, then waited for Arthur to finish.

"Yes. What are we going to do? I mean, if . . . ?" Arthur asked.

Lane waited.

"I mean if Martha doesn't make it?" Arthur's eyes filled with tears. He used a paper napkin to wipe them.

"Then, we take care of Matt, I guess," Lane wiped a non-existent speck off his black-wool slacks.

Arthur touched the side of Lane's face. "Thank you."

Lane shrugged.

"And I'm worried about Mrs. Smallway," Arthur said.

"What? She's got another party planned?"

"No. Well, maybe she does. She talked to Matt the other day. Apparently, when she was on Bobbie's radio show, you were the main topic of conversation whenever they were off the air."

An hour later, Lane and Harper met for coffee at the coffee shop on Kensington. Bryan, the manager of the coffee shop, with the blond-tipped and gelled hair, stood behind the counter. Bryan said, "The usual. A Rolo and and a regular. Black."

Harper said, "You got it." They sat down by the window. Outside, the traffic was lined up to the traffic lights more than a block away. Tail lights glowed an eerie red in the sunrise orange.

Harper pulled a folding keyboard from his pocket, set it on the table, and folded it open.

"It seems like every time I see you, you've got a new piece of equipment," Lane said.

"It seems like every time I see you, you've got bigger circles under your eyes. Anyway, this baby has a camera and voice recorder along with word processing. After we interviewed Jay, I realized this will come in handy the next time we need to record a conversation."

Lane laughed. "Does it dance?"

"No but you can dance if you want. It plays music, and it's wireless."

"Here you go." Bryan slid their coffees onto the table.

"Thanks." *Thank god for coffee,* Lane thought.

"No problem." Bryan left.

"We need to go back over what we've done so far, to see what we've missed." Lane lifted his coffee and closed his eyes with the pleasure of that first sip of the morning.

The screen flickered on Harper's new toy. He leaned forward. "It's all here. I downloaded the information last night. Remember the minister's wife? We haven't seen her yet. First on the list."

Lane said, "Good place to start. And, what about Jay Krocker's lawyer? I've got more questions I'd like to ask the kid. We'll have to run that by the lawyer first."

"Got his number here." Harper pointed and smiled.

Lane decided Harper was just a big kid with his new toy.

Harper typed, sipped his coffee, and scrolled down his notes. "Two question marks here."

"Question marks?" Lane asked.

"You know, when we think we're not getting all of our questions answered, I put a question mark." Harper turned the screen so Lane could see them.

Lane said, "Idaho Metals?"

"Remember how nervous the woman behind the counter was? Her name was Joan."

"And his was Mike," Lane said.

"That's right."

"You're right, she was way too uptight. What's the other question?" Lane asked.

"The case," Harper said.

Lane heard the nervous tension in Harper's voice.

Harper said, "You started out being sure that Bobbie was responsible. Isn't that dangerous? I mean, if we start out thinking one person is guilty, then we may only see the evidence that makes our case."

Lane thought, *How can I explain that I just knew? I knew Bobbie was guilty in a way I can't define. I lived with someone a lot like Bobbie. I knew when I saw Cole, when I saw that sanitized kitchen. I knew some-*

thing was wrong there. "Almost everything we've found out has pointed at Bobbie. The deaths of her parents. The fire in Jamaica. The destruction of a perfectly good car. Eddie. And, don't forget about what Jay had to say without any prompting on our part."

"You have to admit, Eddie's connection is pretty thin," Harper said.

"Not if the DNA comes back as a match," Lane said.

"I'm just saying we've got to be patient."

"You're right," Lane said and thought, *I know in my bones there's something really twisted about Bobbie, but I can't tell Harper that, I can't tell anyone that because then it would mean I'd have to explain why.*

"You're sweating."

Lane took out a handkerchief and wiped his forehead. "It's hot in here."

"You call the minister's wife, and I'll call the lawyer. We'll see what we can set up for today," Harper said.

"What about the auto wreckers?"

"They're next on the list," Harper said.

An hour later, through light traffic, they travelled northwest out of the downtown core. Harper drove.

"What were her directions again?" Harper asked.

"Go along John Laurie. Pass the sign by the church. Take the next right," Lane said.

"Can't believe it took that long to get a hold of her. Who could be stuck on the phone for that long?" Harper asked.

"There's the sign," Lane said.

They read this side of the sign: *Evil cannot touch me because I walk at the right hand of God.*

Lane looked back and read the other side as they passed.

"What's it say?" Harper asked.

"Friends of Bobbie show your support," Lane said.

"What's that mean?" Harper turned right.

"I don't know. We go up the hill, take a right and then another," Lane said.

Within two minutes, they pulled up next to a green two-storey house with lightning rods on the roof. They got out to walk the paved trail leading to a cluster of evergreens. Within the shelter of the trees, there was a bench. A black-haired woman sat there and studied them as they approached. She wore a blue-nylon winter jacket. It was open at the front, revealing a white blouse to go with her grey skirt. Lane guessed her age between thirty-five and forty.

"Mrs. Whyte?" Harper asked.

"Mary," she said.

"This is Lane and I'm Harper."

"Sit down gentlemen," she said. They sat on either side of her. "So, you've tracked down the anonymous Jamaica tip."

"It was a reasonable conclusion." Lane turned slightly to watch her eyes. They were green and looked directly back at him.

"You must be wondering, then, why I didn't meet you at the church or at my home." Mary tucked her black hair behind her ears and looked at each of them.

She shivered, tucked her hands between her knees, and took a deep breath.

"Yes," Lane said.

"There's a phone blitz going on. People have gathered at the church to phone the police stations in a show of support for Bobbie," she said.

"So, that's what the sign was all about," Harper said.

"That's right." Mary looked south toward the downtown core. Her hands shook as she tried to do up the zipper on her coat.

"We have some other questions," Lane said.

"I thought you might," Mary said.

"Your call directed us to investigate Bobbie, and her trip to Jamaica," Lane said.

"That's right. One of the parishioners came to me after the trip. She was one of winners who went along. Apparently, some of the women got involved with the men at the resort. Bobbie was one of them," Mary said.

"What was the parishioner's name?" Harper asked.

Mary said, "I'd rather not say. She was trying to figure out the contradiction of Bobbie's actions at the resort with her radio-personality image. My source would face reprisals if her name got out."

"You know this for a fact?" Lane asked.

"Bobbie has many followers in our church. A year ago, a woman came to me. She showed me a scar on her arm. It was from an old burn. She'd been in junior high school with Bobbie. Apparently, the burn was punishment. Bobbie had ordered her to ostracize another student. The woman said no. She reported that Bobbie burned her. No one would believe it. After the woman told me the story, she left the church." Mary pulled the zipper to her chin and tucked hands into pockets.

"The stories are what we call hearsay," Harper said.

"Since Bobbie joined the church five years ago, the congregation has grown. Every now and then, one of the families will leave. Sometimes, when I call to ask why, I'm told about vague threats made by Bobbie. Very difficult to prove, but threats nonetheless. Again, it's easier to leave the parish than to call the police," Mary said.

"Have you discussed this with your husband?" Harper asked.

"He thinks it's all gossip and innuendo," Mary said.

"So, why are you talking with us?" Harper asked.

"Cole," Mary said.

"Cole Reddie?" Lane asked.

"Yes. He used to play with my son. He told me once that his mother would torture their dog. Bobbie overheard us, and that was the last time the boys played together. Cole is a very bright child. If the stories about Jamaica are true, if Kaylie was not killed by her father, then Cole is in danger." Mary looked directly at Lane. "If something happens to that child, then his blood is on my hands."

Harper said, "One more thing. This phone blitz that's going on. Can you tell us more?"

"One of Bobbie's friends stood up in church yesterday to tell us that Bobbie had been through enough. It was time for the congregation to do what it could to stop Bobbie's nightmare. We were encouraged to phone the police and say it was time to let Bobbie heal," Mary said.

"Oh." Harper looked at Lane.

Lane stood.

"There's one other question you should ask at this point," Mary stood up between them. She looked from side to side and waited.

Harper shrugged.

Lane said, "I'm not sure what you mean."

"Bobbie's friends only act after they first check with Bobbie. I've watched them for a year. Bobbie orchestrated the phone-in. Be certain of that."

Mary walked away from them.

Lane and Harper walked back to the car. Harper drove the Chevy toward the city centre. They crested a hill. The golds and oranges of autumn had almost disappeared, leaving behind a soft haze of brown. The city's colours were leaving for the winter.

Harper said, "See what I mean. We've got lots of something but a whole lot of nothing. About all we got from that is some corroboration for the vet."

"And we've got up to seven deaths attributed to Bobbie," Lane said.

"Or none," Harper said.

"Exactly."

"So, where does that leave us?" Harper asked.

"Looking for more evidence," Lane said.

The phone rang ten minutes later, as they crossed the river.

"Hello?" Lane said. "Yes, Chief." He raised his eyebrows and looked at Harper.

The chief said, "We've logged a little over four-hundred calls this morning. Each one encouraging us to close the Reddie case. All of the calls appear to originate from the same general location."

"At and near Bobbie's church," Lane said.

"Sounds about right," the chief said. "This volume of support and reaction is unprecedented. It appears that our suspect may not be as clever as first indicated. Orchestrating this much pressure aimed at closing a case may be more of an indication of guilt than innocence. You and Harper are the investigators. What you're doing is making someone uncomfortable. Keep it up."

"All right," Lane said.

Twenty minutes later, Harper parked behind a Vietnamese restaurant on Centre Street. "All this fresh air sure works up an appetite." Harper got out of the car.

Lane's phone rang. They stood in the parking lot. Lane listened and pointed at the car with his left hand. Harper climbed back inside.

Lane opened his door and said, "Remember the school down the road from Bobbie's house? Cole Reddie has just been reported missing."

Harper used the lights and siren, while manoeuvring along narrow inner-city streets. When they made it to the boulevard, he opened it up. Ten minutes later, they pulled up in front of Saint Fatima Elementary. It was a brick and red-roofed, single-storey elementary school. They'd seen four police cruisers within a couple of blocks of the school. Now two were parked in front and a police van blocked the entrance to the parking lot. An officer spotted Lane and Harper. He eased the van forward. They pulled into the parking lot between the school and the community's outdoor hockey rink. Sergeant Stephens greeted them. "Hello you two."

"What have you got?" Lane stepped out of the Chevy.

"Not much." Stephens stood almost as tall as Lane. Her auburn hair was braided and tucked up under her cap. "Officers are searching the hills and trees." She indicated a pair of hills rising about seventy-five metres behind the school. Two officers were visible on a trail running between the hills. "The principal is waiting inside to talk with you. Apparently, Cole was playing there." She pointed at the playground at the base of the hill to the west. "He left when a man appeared up there." Stephens pointed up along a path leading to the top of the hill.

"Where's the office?" Lane asked.

"Through the doors, past the gym, and on the right," Stephens said.

Harper opened the side door. They heard the sound of children playing in the gym as they passed. The principal was waiting when they entered the office. He had a round face to match a round body. His hair was thick and black, like the plastic rims of his glasses. "Jack

O'Malley." The principal held out his hand.

Lane and Harper shook hands and introduced themselves.

"Sammy is in my office. He and Cole were on the playground." O'Malley guided Harper and Lane into his office.

Sammy sat with his hands on the arms of the chair. His red hair was cut short. He looked up when they entered the office. His eyes opened wider.

"Hello," Lane said.

"Hi." Sammy swung his feet back and forth while waiting for the detectives to sit down in the chairs arranged around a circular table.

"You were on the playground with Cole?" Harper asked.

"Yes." Sammy studied his white running shoes.

"Can you tell us what you saw?" Lane asked.

"Okay," Sammy said.

Lane waited. Harper followed his lead.

"We were playing on the monkey bars. Then he was going up the hill. Someone was waiting for him on the hill." Sammy stuck his hands in the pockets of his black pants.

"Did the person call Cole's name?" Lane asked.

"Don't know," Sammy said.

"What did this other person look like?" Lane asked.

Sammy frowned and shrugged.

O'Malley said, "Mrs. Dakin is Sammy's teacher. I'm going to ask her to join us."

Lane was about to disagree when Harper smiled

and said, "That would be a good idea."

Mrs. Dakin looked to be about fifty years old. Her hair was cut short, and her eyes were red from crying. She wiped her nose, looked at the officers, and bent down to hug Sammy who immediately began to cry. It took five minutes before the child could speak again. Mrs. Dakin glared at the officers. "Sammy's scared you're going to take him to jail. Tell him he's done nothing wrong."

Harper said, "Of course he's done nothing wrong. Sammy, we just need you to tell us what you remember, so we can find Cole."

Mrs. Dakin said, "Sammy? They just need your help. Can you remember anything else?"

Sammy sniffed and wiped his sleeve across his nose. "The man on the hill waved at Cole."

Lane said, "What was he—"

Mrs. Dakin stopped Lane with another glare. She lifted the boy up and sat him on her knee. "It's okay, Sammy. You just tell us what you saw and we'll listen."

Lane thought, *This teacher knows what she's doing. And, she's a tiger.*

Sammy looked out the window and put his hands on Mrs. Dakin's arm. "We were playing on the monkey bars. I was at the top. I looked for Cole. He was running up the hill. He went to the top of the hill, and the man picked him up. Cole looked back at me and waved. I think he was smiling. Then, they were gone."

"Do you remember anything else about the man?" Mrs. Dakin asked.

"Black hair," Sammy said.

Mrs. Dakin said, "Thank you, Sammy. The boys and girls in class are worried about you. Can you go back and show them you're okay?"

"Okay." he squirmed off her lap and went out the door.

"If he tells us any more, I'll call you. Have you got a card?" Mrs. Dakin asked.

Lane and Harper handed her their cards.

"I need to talk with you about Cole," Mrs. Dakin said.

"This is not the proper time," Mr. O'Malley said.

Mrs. Dakin said, "I couldn't agree less. I've been concerned about Cole for some time now."

Lane asked, "How's that?"

"His mother often takes him to the doctor. He goes to the doctor feeling well and comes back to class not feeling very well at all. Also, he has drawn some worrisome pictures of what's been happening to the family dog."

"Mrs. Reddie is a respected member of the community and a good Christian!" Mr. O'Malley said.

"So? It's Cole I'm worried about. He's been withdrawing inside himself," Mrs. Dakin said.

"Mrs. Dakin!" O'Malley said.

"Oh shut up, Jack! The old church code of hiding the ugly truths isn't going to save this child!" Mrs. Dakin said.

"The child's upset because his sister and father are dead!" O'Malley said.

"Cole was like this before his sister died! I've never seen a child so devoid of hope!" Mrs. Dakin glared at each of the men in turn.

Harper looked at Lane who was transfixed by what Mrs. Dakin was saying.

"I've been doing this for a lot of years," Mrs. Dakin said. "There's something wrong with the way that mother treats her son. What are you going to do about it?"

"Go home! Mrs. Dakin take the rest of the day off! You're hysterical! Get out of my office!" O'Malley wiped the spit from his lips.

There was pounding on the door. It opened.

"Where's my Cole!" Bobbie cried.

A camera light glared over her shoulder.

Lane squinted and put his hand up to shade his eyes.

A reporter asked, "Any comment detective?"

+ + +

It was ten o'clock. Martha watched the news with Lane. She sat across from him, wrapped in a comforter. Her greying hair reached to her shoulders. Martha turned her thinning face to Lane. The latest saga of the Reddie story appeared on television. Riley lay between them on the floor.

The voice-over said, "It appears that Bobbie Reddie's son was abducted today. Ms. Reddie went to her son's school to demand answers."

The camera had caught Lane. He raised his hand to protect his eyes from the intense lights.

The camera turned to Bobbie. She asked, "Where's my boy? What have you done with my son? How could you let my Cole disappear? Haven't I been through enough?" Bobbie spotted Mrs. Dakin who watched Bobbie warily. "I want my son!"

The face of a twenty-something blond reporter appeared. "As yet, there is no news concerning the whereabouts of Cole Reddie, Ms. Reddie's sole-surviving child. This is Alena Zarena for V Channel News."

Lane pressed the remote. The screen went black.

"My, my, my," Martha said.

"What?" Lane asked.

"Bobbie keeps saying "My." It's odd, that's all." Martha shifted her body. She winced with pain.

"You all right?" Lane asked.

"They had to start the chemotherapy too soon after the mastectomy. The cancer's too far along. The doctor said we have to pull out all the stops. God told me to listen to the doctor."

"How come it was left so long?" Lane asked.

"Alex, my husband, said the lump was nothing. He said God would take care of me. Then I found out he was sleeping with someone from the church. That's when we came here. God told me to bring Matt here and go to the hospital."

Lane looked at Riley. The retriever wagged his tail and yawned. "Arthur said the lawyer called today."

"Yes. He said Alex is threatening to take Matt away if I ask for half of his assets. I prayed, and God told me to take the bastard for all he's worth!" Martha said.

Riley closed one eye and cocked his head to the right to get a better look at Martha. The dog licked his lips.

Lane thought, *Matt, you've really got your hands full. A mother who talks with God, a father who uses you as a bargaining chip, and a pair of uncles who are an abomination before the Lord.*

"I know what you're thinking. You think I'm making it up about talking with God."

"You know, it's very dangerous to try and read someone else's mind," Lane said.

"What are you going to do about the child?" Martha asked.

"You mean Matt?" Lane asked.

Martha smiled, "Well, now that you mention it, him too."

+ + +

"Lane! Wake up! You're having a nightmare!" Arthur said.

Lane opened his eyes. He could feel his heart pounding. His ears were ringing with a child's screams. The child had been behind a locked door. Lane had used his heel to kick the solid-core door open. The screams stopped. Lane reached for a light switch. The child was on the wall. Nails had been driven though its hands and feet. Blood dripped onto a green garbage bag on the floor.

"Lane?" Arthur said.

Tuesday, October 27

Chapter 19

"SO, ALL WE'VE got is a big mess," Harper said.

They sat across from one another at the Kensington coffee shop. Bryan, as usual, was getting them a second cup.

"The Police Commission is questioning the chief. Cole's teacher, Mrs. Dakin, gets a week off—maybe more—so she can be the scapegoat. Bobbie has an alibi; she was at work. It looked like we were building a case against her. Now, it looks like our case might be down the toilet," Harper said.

"Go ahead. Say I told you so." Lane's mind was fuzzy from lack of sleep.

"You boys look a little worse for wear." Bryan slid their new coffees over and took the empty mugs.

"You don't know the half of it," Harper said.

"I watch TV. I know some of it," Bryan said.

"Like what?" Harper asked.

"I know you've got this town talkin'," Bryan said.

"That's for sure." Harper cocked his head in the direction of a nearby table. A patron held up the newspaper. The headline screamed **BOBBIE'S SON ABDUCTED.**

Lane looked outside. "We've got to get in touch with Jay."

+ + +

Rush hour traffic was lighter now. The sun had been

down for at least an hour. Lane looked across the street and waited for the crosswalk light to change.

Harper looks as bad as I feel, Lane thought.

"I thought yesterday was bad. Today we accomplished nothing. It seems like the whole case has dried up. Jay's lawyer, Tommy Pham, isn't gonna help, we can't find out who Pham works for, and the DNA tests won't be in for at least another day. Man, this is getting really depressing." Harper stood next to his partner on the street corner.

Lane shook his head. Harper was right.

"You've got a hockey game tonight?" Harper asked.

"Martha's coming," Lane said.

"How's she doing?" Harper asked.

"I'm not too sure."

The light turned green. They stepped into the crosswalk.

"At least the game will be a distraction," Harper said.

Lane took a couple of quick turns on the fresh ice before setting the nets down and making sure everything was in place. He glanced over to the end of the rink where the Zamboni was parked in its garage on the other side of the boards. The rink attendant, Cheryl, gave a wave. Lane waved back and looked into the stands. Arthur and Martha sat side by side. They were deep in conversation and gave him no notice. Behind them, Mac wore his black leather coat and leaned against the railing with one leather-gloved hand over the other. Mac wore a pair of sunglasses and turned his head to glare at Lane while Matt lead the team onto the ice.

Again, Lane was the only referee. Matt played his usual shutout style till there were less than ten minutes to go. After an icing call, the face-off was in Matt's end. Lane dropped the puck, and the centre fed it back to his defenceman who one-timed a shot in the general direction of the net. The puck should have gone wide. Lane watched it deflect off a defenceman's foot. Matt lunged, stumbled, and dove for the puck. It tipped off the end of his trapper and dribbled over the line. Lane pointed and blew the whistle to indicate a goal.

A cheer erupted from the opposing players' bench.

Lane leaned over to get the puck.

The defenceman said to Matt, "Sorry, man."

Matt said, "Don't worry about it."

"Hey goalie! You're useless!"

Lane looked up into the crowd. Arthur was looking over his shoulder. Martha stood up.

Mac said, "No wonder we can't win a game. We got a fudge-packer for a ref, and Quasimodo in net!"

Lane skated toward the boards.

Martha stood one row down from Mac. Mac looked down at her and laughed. Even with her winter coat on, she looked like she weighed less than Mac's leather coat. She reached up to grab Mac's sleeve.

"Let go, bitch!" Mac reached down and grabbed a handful of Martha's hair.

The arena was suddenly and completely silent.

Cheryl ran along the aisle at the top of the stands.

Martha pulled away.

A handful of hair came out in Mac's hand. He held the dangling trophy and smiled. "Nice hair, bitch!"

Lane skated to the gate and opened it.

Arthur moved in between Martha and Mac.

Lane watched Mac swing a fist that hit Arthur in the face.

"Hurry up!" Matt pushed Lane from behind.

Lane climbed the steps.

Arthur fell to one knee and cupped his hands to hold the blood from his nose.

Mac cocked his arm to strike again, but Cheryl grabbed him from behind.

Mac sank to his knees.

Cheryl held his right hand back at an awkward angle. She looked at Lane, "Call the cops."

"Do you want me to take him?" Lane asked.

"You know Hapkido?" Cheryl asked.

"No." Lane thought, *She's got this under control.*

"Then you'd better call," she said.

Mac said, "What did I do? The bitch came after me! I got a right to defend myself."

"Shut up." Cheryl put more pressure on Mac's wrist.

"Shit! You're hurting me!" Mac looked up at Lane. "Do something! She's breaking my arm!"

Lane looked at Mac's face. His eyes were invisible behind the sunglasses. His cheeks were clean-shaven.

Mac looked inconsequential on his knees.

Mac said, "Man, you saw it. I had to defend myself. Those two came after me! It was me or them!"

Lane shook his head and looked back at Arthur. Martha held a wad of bloody Kleenex to his nose. There was a bare patch on the side of Martha's head where Mac had pulled her hair out.

"You okay?" Cheryl said to Martha.

"Chemo," Martha said.

"Had a mastectomy ten years ago, and I'm still around. Smokin' weed helps with the nausea," Cheryl said as if their present circumstances were more like a discussion over coffee in the kitchen than a brawl in an arena.

"What the fuck are you talkin' about?" Mac asked.

"Breast cancer, you asshole!" Cheryl said.

Lane looked around and spotted a woman who was talking on her cellphone. She nodded at Lane, "I've got the police on the line."

Mac said, "The cops won't do a thing to me! I didn't do anything! I'm the victim here!"

Lane turned back to the man, "Since neither of them retaliated, it's not a consensual fight. Quite simply, it's assault. I'm looking forward to saying that in court. You might even get some jail time when she—" Lane pointed at Martha— "testifies. By then she will have no hair at all. Bet it'll even make the papers. Big Mac beats up on a woman with cancer. Your face will be on the news. You'll be famous around town! With any luck, the story will go national."

"Whose side are you on, man?" Mac asked.

Lane thought, *Typical bully. Play the victim.* Lane closed his eyes and saw Bobbie pushing her way into the principal's office. He heard Martha's voice saying, "My, my, my," when she heard Bobbie on television. He saw Mac hitting Arthur in the face, then Mac playing the victim. He saw the look of terror in Cole's eyes. Then, he remembered the nightmare with the crucified child. The flash of insight made him shake his head, take a breath, and open his eyes just so he could be sure he was still in the arena. *Finally,* he thought, *I know exactly what kind of game Bobbie is playing.*

Wednesday, October 28

Chapter 20

HARPER SAID, "SO Arthur's got a pair of black eyes, Martha's lost a chunk of hair, and the rink rat is offering advice on smokin' weed while holdin' this guy in a Hapkido death grip! Then the guys in uniform show up. They couldn't wait to tell their story when they got back downtown. You really know how to get everyone talkin'. I mean this one made its way around the city in record time. Bet the chief's even heard it by now. The guy who thumped Arthur is still in jail! Hear he almost fainted when he found out you were a cop!" He started to laugh, again.

"Especially when I reminded him of what he'd called me." Lane smiled.

"What?" Harper asked, immediately serious.

"Fudge-packer."

"That's not funny," Harper said.

"You didn't see his face." Lane began to chuckle. "Always wanted to do that. You know, tell some macho man I was a cop after he made a homophobic remark. It felt great!"

"You two look a lot happier this morning." Bryan slid their Kensington coffees onto the table.

"Oh, our lives are still in the toilet," Harper said.

A customer called Bryan's name and he left.

"Maybe not," Lane said.

"How so?" Harper asked.

"Bobbie's still our prime suspect. We just have to find Cole," Lane said.

"Lately we haven't had good luck finding live ones, in case you hadn't noticed," Harper said.

"There's something different about this disappearance. Think about it. Cole wasn't dragged away kicking and screaming. Cole went up that big hill to meet the person who took him away. It's almost like Cole was being rescued. And Bobbie's going wild. She was calm and cool when Kaylie disappeared. This time, she's pounding on doors and bringing TV cameras. We need to get some answers from Jay. He seems to know the most about this case."

"What about Charles' sister, Denise?" Harper asked.

"Right now, Jay's our best lead, and he's hard to find," Lane said.

"That's why Steve is coming to meet us," Harper said.

"Steve?"

"Steve Nguyen. He knows all there is to know about the Vietnamese community. He'll have some answers. He'll know who the lawyer, Tommy Pham, works for," Harper said.

Bryan slid a couple of cinnamon buns onto the table. "On the house."

"Nice," Harper said.

Lane pulled out a ten dollar bill. "Sorry, we have to pay."

"It's a special today. Free cinnamon buns." Bryan

looked around the coffee shop.

Lane looked over his shoulder. The husband and wife near the fireplace were buttering their cinnamon buns and smiling at Bryan.

"Thanks," Harper said.

Lane's face reddened as he shoved the bill back in his pocket.

"Uncle Tran," Bryan said.

"What?" Lane asked.

"Tommy Pham works for Uncle Tran. Everybody knows that," Bryan said.

"You know this guy?" Harper asked.

Bryan said, "My parents think he's some kind of saint. Came to Canada before the Vietnamese boat-people started to arrive from the refugee camps. Helped get them settled. Got them places to live. Paid for their education. One of the first kids he put through school was Tommy Pham. Now Tommy handles all of Uncle Tran's legal matters. Come on guys, you didn't notice I'm Asian?" Bryan smiled and turned his head so they could better appreciate his profile.

Harper laughed.

Lane asked, "You know where we can find Uncle Tran?"

"Lucky Elephant Restaurant. In Chinatown. Look for the shortest guy there. It'll be Uncle Tran. But treat him with respect. I'm not kidding. Man's a saint," Bryan said.

A uniformed officer entered the coffee shop. "Here's Steve," Harper said.

Lane watched as recognition washed over Bryan's face. He smiled at Steve. Lane thought, *Bryan and Steve are well acquainted.*

Steve, dressed in his blues, was more than six feet tall. His black hair was cut close. He adjusted the pistol on his hip and made no indication he knew Bryan.

"Good to see you, man." Harper shook hands with Steve. "This is Lane."

Harper smiled at Steve who did not smile back.

"Lane," Steve said and shook hands with Lane before sitting down.

"Want a coffee?" Bryan asked.

"Black." Steve didn't look at Bryan.

Lane took it all in, sat back, and watched Steve as Bryan left. *Steve really has his back up about something,* Lane thought.

Harper glanced at his partner, then said, "We're looking for information on a lawyer called Tommy Pham."

"I know Tommy," Steve said.

"Here's your coffee." Bryan's bonhomie had evaporated.

Steve took a sip, "Good stuff."

"Can you help us?" Harper asked.

Steve said, "Man, you're putting me in a tough spot. We're cops, but this is one hell of a favour. The guy you're looking for put me and my sister through school. Got my mom started in her business."

Harper waited.

Lane watched as Steve looked around the shop,

checking out the clientele one by one.

"You don't understand," Steve said.

"Look, forget we asked. Enjoy your coffee. You and Harper have got some catching up to do. I've got a call to make." Lane got up and left the table. He went to the back of the shop, pulled out his phone, and dialed. "Arthur?"

"Yes," Arthur said.

"Just wanted to talk for a couple of minutes." Lane watched Bryan, who kept an eye on all of the patrons except for Steve.

Steve avoided eye contact with Bryan.

"Martha made an appointment with a hairdresser to see what can be done in the way of damage control," Arthur said.

"How about you?" Lane watched Steve take a sip of coffee, get up, and shake hands with Harper.

"I'm fine. I don't think the nose is broken, but it looks like I'll have two black eyes," Arthur said.

"Go see Dr. Keeler just in case." Lane watched Steve leave. Harper looked at Lane and shrugged.

"Got an appointment before lunch," Arthur said.

"Good. Looks like today might be a long one," Lane said.

"Bye," Arthur said.

Lane walked back to the table and sat down to try another taste of cinnamon bun. "What the hell happened there?"

Harper said, "Beats me. Steve froze up like a lake in winter. It was totally out of character. I mean the guy usually talks my ear off. Man, I'm sorry."

Lane looked over his shoulder. Bryan was behind the counter. The hissing steam of the expresso machine filled the shop. "Don't be. Let's drop in on Charles' sister, Denise. You haven't met her yet. She seems to know Bobbie really well. Maybe she knows something about Cole's disappearance. Then we'll go for lunch at the Lucky Elephant."

It took fifteen minutes to reach the apartment across from Buckmaster Park. The sun was just up. It warmed their faces as they walked across the street, went downstairs, and knocked on Denise's door.

She opened it after a minute. Denise had a cup of coffee in her right hand. Her left went to close the neck of her white blouse. "It's cold. Come on in." She backed up.

Lane thought Denise looked older than the last time they had met. The circles under her eyes were darker. Lane noticed the belt holding up her slacks was cinched two stops past the line worn in black leather.

The detectives crowded into the tiny apartment.

"Want a coffee?" Denise asked.

"No thank you. Just a couple of questions," Lane said.

Denise leaned up against the frame of the kitchen doorway. "Want to look around?"

"Sure." Harper stepped past her and into the bedroom.

"You must want to know where Cole is. I wish I knew. He's a good kid. Never said much, but he was always a kind kid," Denise said.

"Was?" Lane asked.

"What do you think the chances are?" Denise's voice was all at once resigned and bereft.

"Actually, I wanted to know if you've ever met Jay Krocker," Lane said.

"Bobbie's brother, Jay?" Denise asked.

"Yes," Lane said.

"Only ever saw him at the kids' birthday parties. Usually up until the point his sister said something nasty and he left." Denise watched Harper as he moved into the living room.

Lane waited.

Harper looked at Lane and shook his head to indicate there was no one else in the apartment.

"Jay was a nice kid. Real short attention span. Maybe that's why Cole and Kaylie always hung off of him. When he was around, Cole would talk nonstop whenever Bobbie left the room. Jay sure had a knack for bringin' Cole out of his shell. Kaylie adored him too. Charles wished Jay would come around more often," Denise said.

"We'd like to talk with Jay," Lane said.

"No idea where he lives. Bobbie had no idea either. She used to interrogate him about it every time they met. But he never would tell her where he lived," Denise said.

"Have you got any idea where Cole might be?" Lane asked.

Denise said, "Been up all night thinking about it.

Just hope he doesn't turn up like his sister and father." She shuddered and her head dropped. Denise leaned away from the door frame and stood straight. "I've got to get to work. As you can see, unfortunately, Cole's not here."

They killed two hours checking over details downtown. At 11:15 AM they walked to Chinatown and found The Lucky Elephant Restaurant. It was about a block from the river and just across the street from the red-bricked federal building. The sun was bright. Lane and Harper passed a few people who were wearing shorts and T-shirts. The joggers headed down the sidewalk toward the trails along the river.

A bell sounded as they opened the door of The Lucky Elephant Restaurant. They stepped inside and looked around. Four tables were filled with office workers who'd decided on an early lunch.

In the corner, a white-haired man waved to them. He sat with his back to the wall. He stood. He wore a red golf shirt and black jeans.

Lane noted the man's table offered him the best vantage point in the room.

Lane and Harper approached and stopped across the table from the white-haired man. He offered his hand first to Lane, "Mr. Lane and Mr. Harper, I'm Lam Tran. Most people call me Uncle Tran." After shaking Harper's hand, Uncle Tran said, "Please sit."

Harper looked at Lane. The older detective raised his eyebrows and thought, *Just go with it.*

Lane noted Uncle Tran had an accent, but his

English was very good. Instinctively, Lane knew he was sizing up an extremely intelligent man. Lane pulled out a chair and said, "News certainly travels fast."

"Canadian cities are still quite small by Asian standards. News certainly does travel fast," Uncle Tran said.

A waiter arrived, set down two menus and poured water for Uncle Tran, Lane, and Harper.

"Today, I'd suggest the curried beef with mixed vegetables," Uncle Tran said.

"Sounds very nice," Lane said.

Harper studied the menu. "Me too."

"We've been told you're a saint," Lane took a sip of water.

"An exaggeration," Uncle Tran smiled.

Lane had made a point of sitting across from Uncle Tran so he could watch the man's eyes. "I'm impressed with the way you knew us even before we introduced ourselves."

Uncle Tran looked directly back at Lane. "Wherever you are, it helps to have friends."

Lane thought, *It was probably Steve who let Tran know we were looking for him. I wonder if Harper knows.*

Harper smiled, "We would like to get in touch with Jay Krocker."

"You get right to the point. It's the best approach. I will pass on a message to him if you wish," Uncle Tran said.

Lane thought, *Think carefully about this.*

The waiter arrived with three plates and a large red plastic container of steamed rice.

Uncle Tran picked up his chopsticks, chose a piece of beef and dipped it into the curry sauce. He put the morsel in his mouth and closed his eyes with pleasure.

"That was quick service." Harper tried to pick up the chopsticks, then put them down and reached for a fork.

Lane used chopsticks to select a morsel of red pepper along with a piece of beef and put them in his mouth. The curry was sweet and hot, the beef tender, and the pepper crisp. He had never tasted curry like this in his life. He chewed and said, "Magnificent."

Uncle Tran smiled, "It is quite delicious. Hard to get a curry dish this wonderful in the west."

Harper coughed. Lane and Uncle Tran looked at him. Harper's face was red. He reached for a glass of water.

"Wait." Uncle Tran reached for the rice and spooned some onto Harper's plate. "Eat some rice. It will ease the discomfort."

Harper shoveled steamed rice into his mouth. His face turned pink. "Thanks. Man, that's hot!"

"You may wish for something milder," Uncle Tran said.

"Maybe," Harper said.

Uncle Tran motioned for the waiter. "You like chicken?"

"Yes," Harper said.

Uncle Tran said, "Number 53," to the waiter, and then to Harper, "I apologize."

Harper took a gulp of water, swallowed, then sucked some ice into his mouth. Tears ran down his cheeks.

Lane smiled and ate another mouthful of vegetables and beef. *It's really wonderful,* he thought. Sweat broke out on his forehead. His nose began to run.

"We'd like to meet Jay face to face," Harper said.

"Is he to be charged with a crime?" Uncle Tran chewed thoughtfully.

He isn't sweating at all, Lane thought. "We have questions related to a murder investigation."

"Is Jay accused of murder?" Uncle Tran looked right at Lane.

"No, but he may be able to help us solve one," Lane said.

Uncle Tran scooped some rice into the curry sauce at the edge of his plate. "This Jay is a good boy. He protected my nephew, Tony, when their boss was being a bully. Jay went back to help my niece, Rosie, when everyone else ran away. You know this also. I will pass on your message to Jay, but whether or not he will meet you face to face, this is his decision."

Lane took his card out and slid it across the table to Uncle Tran. "It is important he gets in touch with us."

"I understand," Uncle Tran said.

+ + +

Harper took the call as they walked along Seventh

Avenue. The C-Train rumbled by. He had to cup his left hand over his ear to hear the caller. "Hello."

"The DNA canine results are in." The voice was deep and utterly toneless.

"Who is this?" Harper asked.

"Colin Weaver. You requested a match on the canine hairs found on the child's clothing—one Kaylie Reddie, deceased—with the samples from the dog from Dr. Ellen Dent's office."

"That's right." Harper looked at Lane and mouthed the words, "Doctor Fibre."

The C-Train moved on. Harper was able to remove his hand from his ear.

Weaver said, "Dr. Ellen Dent was correct. The samples are a match. They come from the same animal. I'll forward a copy of the report to you."

"Thanks," Harper said.

Weaver muttered something unintelligible, and the line went dead.

Harper said, "Dr. Dent's dog and the samples from Kaylie's clothes are a match."

Lane said, "Good, we're finally getting somewhere."

+ + +

BOBBIE: Good afternoon. It's Bobbie on the ride home. This is a personal appeal to my listeners. Please look at the pictures of my son in the newspapers and on TV. I warned the police this might happen. Now, I'm relying on you to find my only surviving child. I'm hoping to find a way to raise a reward for my son's safe return. The police say they are looking for my son. I choose to put my son's life in your hands.

+ + +

Lane was waiting in traffic at the lights when the phone rang.

"Lane?"

Lane recognized the voice, "Chief."

"One question. At any time during the investigation did Bobbie Reddie warn you of a danger to her son?"

"No, but other witnesses warned us that Bobbie was a danger to her child." Lane turned right onto Glenmore Trail.

"Any leads on the child?" the chief asked.

"One," Lane said.

"Keep on it."

"We will," Lane said.

The Chief of Police hung up.

+ + +

It was 5:30 PM when the knock came on Jay's door. He was sitting in the chair by the window.

The knock came again. "Jay? Come on. It's me, Rosie. Tony's here too."

Jay got up and walked to the door. He looked over his shoulder then put his hand on the doorknob.

"Jay? We've got a message from Uncle Tran," Rosie said.

"Not now." Jay pulled his hand away from the door.

"Look, Jay," Rosie's voice was lower, just loud enough to be heard through the door. "I spoke to the landlady. She told me a story. She says you brought a child to your apartment. You want me to blab it all over? I mean the landlady only speaks Vietnamese, but her eyes are good. I speak English and Vietnamese, so I can blab the story to almost anyone in town. The thing is, even I'm not as nosy as the landlady. Maybe you'd like her to come around and ask the questions?"

Jay opened the door.

Rosie noticed he was wearing black sweats and a blue T-shirt.

"Come in," Jay said.

Rosie walked in, followed by Tony.

Jay closed the door.

They stood there looking at the child asleep on the couch.

Tony said, "Shit! Man, that kid's face is everywhere."

Rosie turned to Jay. "Explain."

"He's my nephew. I went to his school and waited 'til he came out at lunch time. Then I brought him back here." Jay rubbed his eyes.

"Sit down," Rosie said.

Jay sat in the chair across from the couch.

In the silence, they heard Cole's gentle breathing.

"My sister killed Kaylie. Then she killed Cole's dad. Cole saw most of it. He was talking in his sleep last night and most of it came out. No wonder he's afraid to sleep. He thinks his mom will come for him and put him in the trunk of her car like she did Kaylie. He's terrified at night. I can't get any sleep, because he wakes up screaming. He'll only sleep when the sun's up and only if I promise to stay awake while he sleeps. We can't leave the apartment, because someone will recognize him. We're trapped." Jay leaned back in the chair and stared at the ceiling. "I haven't slept since we came here."

Rosie sat down on the couch by Cole's feet.

Tony sat on the floor with his back to the wall. "Man, you should've called us."

"I didn't know what to do," Jay said.

"Get Jay something to drink," Rosie said to Tony.

When the fridge door opened, Rosie said, "The landlady's not a problem. She just saw you bring a boy in here. I asked her to keep quiet. Eventually, someone else will spot Cole. It's only a matter of time before the police come to your door. Besides, there's another problem. Uncle Tran." She rubbed Cole's feet and smiled.

"He's mad at me?" Jay asked.

"No, he's living here illegally. If you get caught and the police find out he's not a Canadian citizen, he'll be deported," Rosie said.

"No way," Jay said.

Tony handed Jay a glass of water. "When Uncle Tran stepped off the airplane, he came to Chinatown, and stayed. He didn't stop at customs and immigration."

Jay took a sip of water. *I need some sleep,* he thought.

Tony said, "Get some sleep. Rosie and I will keep an eye on Cole."

"I don't know what he'll do when he wakes. He doesn't know you." Jay closed his eyes for a few seconds. It was hard for him to open them again.

"We'll take good care of him," Rosie said.

Thursday, October 29

Chapter 21

"WHY AREN'T WE looking for Cole?" Harper asked.

Lane drove in the middle lane of the freeway. The tires hummed on the grooved surface. "His face is everywhere. Bobbie's putting together a reward. If he's alive, he'll turn up. Tommy Pham's phoning us before noon. That gives us time to cruise by Idaho Metals so we can tie up this loose end."

"I'm not sure," Harper said as they passed a van on their right. The driver was singing. He looked over at Harper and smiled.

"I'm not sure either, that's why we're going. We weren't sure about that vet Dr. Dent, and she's looking like an impeccable but quirky source. Remember how nervous junkyard Joan was?"

"I remember. It's just . . ." Harper said.

"What?"

"Bobbie's actions seem so illogical."

"You're right, it's not about logic. It's beginning to look like it's all about ego. If you accept the premise that each of these murders is motivated by ego, then it begins to appear that each murder has some logic behind it." Lane eased off the freeway.

+ + +

Jay woke at eight-thirty in the morning. Someone had

covered him with a blanket. Sunlight streamed in through the curtains. Tony was snoring on the couch.

Jay got up. He heard water running in the bathroom and walked down the hall. He inhaled the sneezy scent of hair-salon products.

Rosie said, "We'll get you some new clothes. When Jay gets up, he'll make you breakfast."

"Are you Uncle Jay's girlfriend?" Cole asked.

"I think we'd have to kiss first." Rosie's tone told Cole any question was reasonable. "Let's dry your hair and see what it looks like."

"Okay," Cole said.

Jay peeked in the door. "Wow," he said.

Rosie and Cole's reflections were framed in the mirror. Rosie rubbed Cole's head with a towel. His hair was red and cut within a centimetre of the scalp. "Rosie's gonna buy me some new clothes," Cole said.

"Well?" Rosie asked.

"He looks totally different." Jay smiled.

Rosie smiled back.

Jay felt like singing. Instead, he said, "I gotta go."

"Where?" There was apprehension in Cole's voice.

"To the bathroom," Jay said.

"Come on Cole, we're all done," Rosie said. They pushed past Jay. Her hair brushed Jay's arm. Rosie smiled at him. Jay caught a whiff of her shampoo. It smelled of citrus and honey.

+ + +

"Will you look at that?" Harper said.

"Sometimes, you just never know." Lane looked at Harper who was smiling.

"Same year, colour, and make. You don't think?" Harper asked. He studied the champagne-coloured Chrysler parked in the Idaho Metals parking lot out front of the office.

"At the very least, it's worth checking out." Lane parked their Chevy directly behind the Chrysler.

They got out of the car and walked up the frost-coated steps to the office. The lights were on inside. Joan looked up when they opened the door. Her face immediately turned red.

Harper said, "Hello, Joan. We were just in the neighbourhood."

Joan picked up her coffee cup.

Lane noticed that her hand was shaking.

She wrapped ten long fingers around the cup. Joan sipped without taking her eyes off them. She glanced at the photo of her sons.

"Is Mike around?" Harper asked.

"Should be here any minute," Joan said. It sounded like she wished Mike would hurry up.

"Would you prefer we waited or could we talk with you now?" Lane asked.

"Up to you." Joan tried to make herself sound nonchalant. It had the opposite effect on Harper.

"Been watching the news?" Harper asked.

"Hard not to," Joan said.

Go easy, Lane thought, *Joan's got two kids. She'll be worried about what will happen to them if we arrest her. Women can be tigers when it comes to protecting their kids.*

"There's a boy missing. You may be in a position to help us and help the kid at the same time," Harper said.

"Really?" Joan said. "Missing people in Bobbie's family have been turning up dead. Families can be dangerous."

"Sounds like you've had a bad experience," Lane said.

"Had a husband who threatened to kill my boys if I left him. He put me in the hospital, just to prove his point. I left him after that. He's in jail now, but he'll be out someday," Joan said.

"And we've got a kid we need to find," Harper said.

"Don't see what that has to do with me." Again, Joan used both hands to lift the coffee cup. She hid her face as she took a sip.

"We need Bobbie's car because it could help us determine if the fibres in the trunk match fibres found on the child's body," Lane said.

Before Joan could answer, Harper said, "We're only interested in the car. If we find the car in question, we'll need it for evidence. The person who has possession of the car will help us establish that it did, in fact, belong to Bobbie Reddie. We won't be looking at charging the new owner."

"Police couldn't protect me before. What makes you think anything's changed?" Joan asked.

Mike opened the door.

Both detectives turned.

Mike studied the faces in the room. He brushed at the front of his coveralls; buying time. He frowned, thought, and smiled. "Want a cup of coffee officers?"

"They know." Joan's shoulders sagged. She looked at Lane. "I never could put groceries in the trunk of that car. I kept thinking about why she wanted the car wrecked. I mean who in her right mind would want to get rid of a car like that? She must have had a reason. I just never opened the trunk. Kept thinking about my twins and what their father threatened to do to them."

Mike said, "Joan's car was on its last legs. We didn't charge Bobbie anything for wrecking her car, just substituted Joan's old one. Bobbie never noticed. She thought she got rid of her car, and Joan got a new one."

"You never opened the trunk?" Lane asked.

"I didn't," Mike said.

Joan said, "Not me. Never worked up the nerve."

"Would you testify that you switched your car for hers but never opened the trunk of Bobbie's?" Lane asked.

"Do we have a choice?" Mike asked.

Harper said, "It's the only choice that I'd make."

"It's right around here." Tony rode up front with Rosie. Jay and Cole sat in the back seat of her Honda.

"There's a parking spot." Rosie pulled up to the curb. "Anybody got any change for the meter?"

"How much you need?" Jay asked, reaching into his pocket.

"Couple of loonies should do it," Rosie said.

"This is crazy. You realize this is nuts. I mean two Asians with a white kid? If we get caught, the news will say we're Asian gang members involved in the white slave trade." Tony smiled when he said it, but his voice was pitched too high.

"Slavery was abolished, at least in North America, at the time of the American Civil War," Cole said.

"As long as we're not arrested for pimping. I'd never live that one down," Rosie said.

"Aren't pimps usually male?" Cole asked.

"Damn, you're just too smart aren't you, Cole?" Tony said.

"What's your new name, Cole?" Rosie asked.

"Chuck," Cole said.

"You guys are crazy," Tony said.

"Everybody's looking for a blond-haired boy in church clothes. Once we get him a ball cap, some baggy pants, and a T-shirt with somethin' obscene on it, nobody'll give him a second look." Rosie checked for traffic and got out.

The boys all stepped onto the sidewalk. Jay felt completely vulnerable.

"Sell it." Rosie took Cole's hand. "Me and Chuck are going shoppin'." Cole looked back over his shoulder to make sure Jay was following.

People on the sidewalk passed without noticing. Cars drove by without stopping.

Rosie, Cole, Jay, and Tony crossed the street. They stepped into the skateboard/snowboard shop. Cole stared at the girl who sat behind the till. She had studs in her eyebrow and lip. When she opened her mouth, there was one in her tongue. Her hair, eyebrows, and clothes were black.

"Got some stuff to fit him?" Rosie asked.

"Right there," the clerk pointed to a corner at the back of the store.

"This looks good," Jay grabbed a red hat.

"How about this?" Tony pulled out a blue T-shirt.

Cole looked at Rosie, who held up a pair of khaki trousers with more pockets than a pool table. The child stood in the middle of the store, overwhelmed. His eyes filled with tears.

Jay got on one knee so he could look Cole in the eyes and asked, "What's the matter?"

"I never picked out my own clothes before," Cole said.

"It can be fun," Rosie said.

"Fun?" Cole asked.

"You know, you try on some stuff and try on some more and have, you know, fun," Tony said.

Cole looked bewildered.

"What if you pick one person to bring you clothes?" the clerk asked.

Everyone turned to look at her.

"Okay," Cole said.

"How about Rosie?" Jay asked.

"Okay." Cole sounded relieved.

Cole ended up with a red hat with the brim pointed forward, a blue T-shirt with a white stripe across the chest, and a pair of green cotton pants with more pockets than the one Rosie had first shown him.

Tony, Jay, and Cole picked up the old clothes in the changing room while Rosie pulled out her card and handed it to the clerk.

The clerk swiped the card and said, "The kid's still recognizable."

Rosie thought she might vomit. "What do you mean?"

"The kid's face is everywhere. It's only a matter of time before somebody goes for the reward." The clerk handed Rosie the receipt.

"What about you?" Rosie signed the receipt.

"You think Bobbie and her fans wanna make the world a better place for people like me? Look at me. I'm just sayin' it's only a matter of time before somebody spots you. The kid looks like he doesn't know what to do with himself. People are actually asking him what he thinks. What he wants. He's not acting like a kid should. He looks like he's been abused. Believe me, I know that look. Take care of that kid. His sister and his dad just died," the clerk said.

"Thanks." Rosie stuffed her copy of the receipt in her purse and waited outside until the boys caught up.

When they were back in the car she asked, "What's the plan, Jay?"

"Plan?" Jay asked.

"We need a plan or we're finished," Rosie said.

Jay looked at Cole, who looked out the window. "Cole?" Jay asked.

Cole turned to face his uncle.

"What happened to Kaylie and your Dad?" Jay asked.

"Mommy said if I told anyone, there'd be a fire," Cole said.

"What's that mean?" Tony asked.

"That my sister'll make somebody pay if Cole tells the truth about Charles and Kaylie," Jay said.

"Uncle Tran was right," Rosie said.

"What are you talkin' about?" Tony asked.

"He called me last night and said the landlady saw you take Cole into the apartment. Then Uncle Tran told me what to do. I called him again while you were asleep. He thought you probably hadn't planned very far ahead. He thinks this won't end until you end it," Rosie said.

"What's that mean?" Jay asked.

"It means the police, Tommy Pham, and Uncle Tran want to see you this afternoon. I'll take care of Cole while you meet them, Jay," Rosie said.

+ + +

Lane followed the tow truck down the freeway. On the deck behind the truck's cab, Bobbie's Chrysler bobbed each time the truck hit a ripple in the pavement.

"Dr. Fibre'll meet us there so he can get started on the forensics." Harper flipped his phone closed.

Lane nodded. He thought about their next move. "Even if the fibres and hairs are a match, it probably won't be enough. We've got to get someone to testify.

With Bobbie, we'll need more rather than less evidence."

"So, we need a witness. And, so far, we've only got two likely candidates," Harper said.

"And both have disappeared. A bit too much of a coincidence," Lane said.

"Talking with Tommy Pham is the next step, then," Harper said.

They got the call thirty minutes later.

+ + +

Lane and Harper sat side by side at the conference table. The clock on the wall showed 5:00 PM. Tommy Pham's office was occupied by a group of lawyers in a renovated house north of the river. The house looked down onto Chinatown. The sun shone in the window, and they squinted at the Lion's Bridge.

"How old is Tommy?" Lane asked.

"Maybe thirty," Harper said.

"So, he's a recent grad," Lane said.

"Where are you goin' with this?" Harper asked.

"It's just that he's doing very well for a lawyer who graduated in the last couple of years," Lane said.

"So?" Harper looked sideways at Lane.

"Uncle Tran runs a restaurant, offers financial aid to the community, and it looks like he set Tommy up in this place." They looked at the oak finish on the walls, solid-oak table, and oak armchairs. "Uncle Tran must sell a tonne of satay."

Tommy opened the door. He was followed by Jay

Krocker and Uncle Tran. The three sat across the table from Lane and Harper.

"Please close the blinds," Harper said.

Tommy pressed a button under the table. A motor whirred. The blinds closed. They made very little difference. Lane and Harper were forced to squint into slightly-shaded sunlight.

Lane smiled and waited. *In times like this,* he thought, *the only thing to do is wait. We're being put at a disadvantage, so we wait. Let them make the next move.*

Harper looked at Lane, then across the table at Tommy who wore a grey suit and red tie.

The silence of the first minute stretched into five.

"I've got an appointment at 5:30," Tommy said.

Lane nodded. He thought, *Pissing contests can be so tedious.*

Uncle Tran smiled. "We have limited time, gentlemen. A child is in danger."

Lane forced himself to sit still and wait some more.

Harper inhaled and leaned forward.

"We would like to know if you are interested in the whereabouts of Cole Reddie?" Tommy asked.

"Of course." Lane watched Jay shift in his chair.

"What will happen to the child if he's released into your custody?" Tommy asked.

"That depends," Lane said.

Harper leaned closer to Lane and said, "Protective custody?"

"We have reason to believe the child will be in

danger if returned to his mother," Tommy said.

"It's very important you be specific with your reasons," Lane said.

Jay looked at Tommy who nodded back.

Jay said, "He talks in his sleep. Cole says, 'Mommy, don't put Kaylie in the trunk. Please Mommy, why won't she wake up?' He says it over and over again." Jay's eyes were all at once pleading and resigned as he looked at the officers. "When I was fifteen, Bobbie burned our house down and killed my parents. I kept quiet because she threatened me and Cole."

"Did she ever confess to you?" Lane asked.

"She told me she was afraid Cole would die in his sleep. I told you this before. It's the way my sister makes threats. She was telling me that Cole would die, if I told anyone that she'd started the fire in my parents' house," Jay said.

"There is another matter. Jay is voluntarily surrendering the child. He has no interest, whatsoever, in the reward offered for the safe return of Cole Reddie. Jay's only interest is in the safety of his nephew. Our interest," Tommy nodded at Uncle Tran, "is in the safety of Cole and Jay."

"Speaking of interests, we're interested in Uncle Tran. So far as I can tell, he doesn't exist," Harper said.

There was a prolonged silence around the table. Uncle Tran smiled.

Tommy looked at Harper as if the cop had just crapped in the punch bowl at the mayor's year-end bash.

Lane thought, *Don't let this fall apart before the*

child is safe! "Right now, our major concern is the safety of Cole and Jay. Both will be placed in custody."

"You are guarantying that both Cole and Jay will be placed in protective custody?" Tommy asked Lane as if Harper had disappeared from the room.

"Jay may be charged with abduction. Whether we like it or not, there are some things beyond our control," Lane said.

Tommy looked at Uncle Tran. Tran shook his head from side to side.

"We need your assurance that Jay will not be charged. His only thought was to protect the child from a deadly situation," Tommy said.

Uncle Tran is one tough negotiator, Lane thought. "I'll need to make some phone calls." Lane got up and motioned for Harper to follow. They stepped outside and closed the door. In the hallway, Lane pulled out his phone and said to Harper, "What the hell did you ask that question for?"

"I can't find any record of Uncle Tran. He doesn't exist," Harper said.

"Next time we're in a situation like this one, leave out questions like that." Lane speed-dialed.

"I don't think we'll be in a situation like this again," Harper said.

They returned five minutes later. Tommy and Uncle Tran were speaking Vietnamese. Jay looked like he had aged a year.

"Both Jay and Cole will be placed in protective custody," Lane said.

Jay took a deep breath.

"Will they be together?" Uncle Tran asked.

"What?" Harper asked.

"While you were outside, we received a call. The child is becoming very agitated without his uncle. Will the child be kept with Jay?" Uncle Tran asked.

"Man you got a pair on you," Harper said.

"What did you say?" Tommy asked.

Uncle Tran smiled.

Lane said, "I'll see to it. Now, where is the child?"

"Will Jay be charged?" Uncle Tran asked.

Lane said, "No. Now, where is Cole?"

"Very close," Tommy said.

+ + +

Lane drove down Centre Street and over the Lion's Bridge. Harper sat in the back with Jay on one side, and Cole in the middle.

The red hair is a nice touch, Lane thought. He noticed the haunted look of the child's eyes.

"I know you," Cole said, looking at Lane.

"Yes, we've met before," Lane said.

"Are you feeling better?" Cole asked.

"Pardon?" Lane asked.

"You got sick outside of my house," Cole said.

"I'm better now." Lane thought, *Jay's right about this kid.*

"Good," Cole said.

They turned east. When they arrived at the station, the cameras and reporters were waiting.

"How'd they know?" Jay asked.

Harper said, "You tell me. Scanner, probably. They listen in on our communications. It's like a game, and they're always up to new tricks. Might as well make the best of it."

"Smile everybody." Lane put the turning signal on and slowed to a crawl.

The car was surrounded by reporters, cameras, and microphones. Lane concentrated on looking ahead and moving forward without running anyone over. The camera flashes were mostly to his right and left, so he wasn't blinded.

Harper, Jay, and Cole weren't as lucky. Cole sat bewildered by the entire experience. One photograph caught Jay attempting to shield his eyes from the lights and camera flashes. It froze his hand over his eyes where it appeared he was attempting to mask his identity. It was not the image which made the evening news, but it did make the morning papers across the country. Then the story went international.

+ + +

BOBBIE: Good afternoon. It's Bobbie on the ride home. My nightmare continues. My son is in police custody. My lawyer is working on his release. My brother, the product of a very disturbed childhood, is under police protection. If the police can do this to me, they can do it to you! My rights as a mother and a woman have been violated!

+ + +

"Remember Lisa's partner, Loraine? She is recommending a meet with Cole and Jay tomorrow. She wants the two of them to relax a bit. She says Cole needs to be near Jay now. If Cole actually saw what we believe he saw, then he needs Jay around." Lane smiled at the ruse they had used to sneak the pair out of downtown and into a condo on the west side of the city. They used a convoy of four identical vans in the middle of rush hour traffic, then drove Cole and Jay away in an unmarked police car when the media chased the vans.

Lane and Harper sat across the table from one another in a small conference room. Harper looked over the top of his laptop. He plugged it into a wall outlet to tap into the Internet. He transferred information from his pocket computer to the larger machine to backup information.

Harper said, "I checked my e-mail. There's a quick note from Dr. Fibre. The chief gave him priority on the evidence from the trunk of Bobbie's car. He's talking about a preliminary report within twenty-four to forty-eight hours. The e-mail from Jamaica is really gonna blow your mind. The police photographed footprints at the murder scene. They've been able to eliminate all but one pair. They've couriered us photographs of both unidentified prints. Should be here tomorrow. They want us to eliminate Bobbie as a suspect."

"No fax?" Lane felt his pulse quicken. Evidence began to pile up in a case that had previously been starved for hard facts.

"Their fax won't pick up the kind of detail we need

for a match. They're in the process of upgrading their equipment. So, they're sending us a copy of the prints from the crime scene photographs," Harper said.

Lane and Harper knew that footprints, like fingerprints were unique to the individual. If they could match Bobbie's footprints to the scene of the three deaths in Jamaica, they might be able to make a case for five murders instead of two.

"The next couple of days will be tough." Lane stood and took off his sports jacket to hang it on the back of the chair beside him. "If Cole will testify, if the fibres in the back of the Chrysler are a match, if the footprints from Jamaica match Bobbie's . . . if we're wrong about any of these pieces. . . ."

Harper locked his hands behind his head, "We're still way ahead of where we were two days ago." He smiled.

+ + +

Darkness settled around his neighbourhood. Lane studied the unmarked car parked on the south side of the street. Two people in the front seat watched Lane as he drove by. His headlights illuminated the garage door. It lifted, and Lane pulled inside.

In less than a minute, his key was in the lock. Arthur opened the door, pulling the keys from Lane's hand.

"We saw you on TV," Arthur said.

"Did you notice the car parked outside?" Lane slipped his shoes off and stepped into the kitchen. Peering into the living room, he saw Matt and Riley curled up on the rug. Matt had his head on a pillow and was asleep. Riley was curled up back-to-back with Matt. The retriever's eyes opened and focused on Lane. Riley's tail lifted itself off the floor then flopped back. "Hello boy." Lane bent down and rubbed the dog behind the ears. Riley sighed and closed his eyes.

Martha was wrapped in a blanket and sitting on the couch. She smiled at Lane. Her head was shaved. Martha kept her voice low as she said, "Matt and Riley went for a walk after supper. They stayed up just long enough to catch you on the news."

Lane smiled at the scene. It was the last thing he would have expected even two months ago. Previously, Arthur and Lane had fallen into a comfortable routine of work, solving cases, and taking Riley for walks. Now they were making plans for Halloween and talking about a Christmas spent with family.

Lane backed into the kitchen and heard Arthur opening the oven door.

"Kept supper warm for you." Arthur used oven mitts to get the plate out and onto a bamboo place mat.

"The car?" Lane asked as he sat down, picking carefully at the aluminum foil covering the food.

"They introduced themselves about an hour ago. They were instructed to tell me that the next few days of this case are critical. Chief wants you to be sure about our safety. You're not to be distracted." Arthur sat down across from Lane.

"Why would I worry about home?" Lane smiled when he thought about Jay and Martha and how this house has been turned upside down. He took a deep breath as he uncovered the chicken and baby potatoes bathed in tomato sauce. "I'm starved." He picked up a fork and knife.

"Don't you remember?" Arthur asked.

"Remember what?" Lane asked.

"Mrs. Smallway was on Bobbie's show. It was last week," Arthur said. "You know what Mrs. Smallway is like. She lives to gossip, and she leaves those underlined articles in our mailbox."

Lane looked at the food on his plate. His appetite disappeared. He thought, *What did Smallway tell Bobbie?* He looked at Arthur.

Arthur was up and looking in at Martha. Without looking at Lane, he said, "The long-range forecast is predicting a major snow storm on Halloween."

Friday, October 30

Chapter 22

CLUES, FACES, AND words swirled around Lane's mind like moths pulled to a porch light. At two o'clock he gave up trying to sleep and went to read in the living room. These past few weeks, this routine had become maddeningly familiar. The only difference was that tonight's sleeplessness was not caused by nightmares of crucified children. Cole was safe for the moment. But, it appeared, everyone and everything else was now at risk.

He put on a housecoat and stepped into the hallway. The furnace hummed and forced air through the vents. A pale glow reflected off the hallway wall.

Martha sat on the couch, wrapped in her yellow blanket, staring at the TV screen. She had the closed-captioning on. There was a head and shoulders shot of a man with perfect hair and perfect teeth. The caption read, "Real power is about becoming the person you were born to be. The person God meant you to be."

He sat across from her.

"Matt has a game tonight. You able to make it?" Martha's voice sounded strong even though the shadows cast by the TV deepened the lines around her eyes and mouth.

"I'm going to try." Lane propped his feet on the coffee table.

"Matt told me you stuck up for him," Martha said.

"Well . . ."

"His father, Alex, never once stuck up for him. After the first couple of hockey games, he was always too busy to make it. Took me a while to understand he was ashamed of Matt and of me. Matt will never forget the first time someone stuck up for him. I only wish it had been me," Martha said.

"Why would Alex be ashamed of either of you?" Lane asked.

"It's hard to explain," Martha said.

"We've got time." Lane smiled.

"It was my fault."

Lane said, "I'm not sure I understand."

"One imperfect child. Matt was a constant disappointment to Alex."

"Why was it your fault?" Lane asked.

"It wasn't, I was just lead to believe that was the case. That's the beauty of cancer. It makes you take stock. It makes you see what's important in life. It's almost like God sent me a gift. I realized that there was no reason for blaming anyone. Matt is just fine the way he is," Martha said.

"That's the difference between you and me," Lane said.

"What? I believe in God and you don't?"

"I just think people are responsible for most of the terrible things done in this world," Lane said.

"So you have given the good Lord some consideration?" Martha sounded triumphant.

"Of course."

"Go ahead. Say it," Martha said.

"Say what?" Lane asked.

"That you'll give yourself over to the Lord. Become his servant."

Lane looked at Martha as if seeing her for the first time. He wondered what was godlike about abandoning your brother and being blissfully unaware of the resultant damage. It had been twenty years since most of Arthur's family had washed their hands of him. Lane had seen how their cruel rejections had scarred Arthur.

"Just be careful you don't run out of time before you give God a chance," Martha said.

Lane said nothing. He was afraid that all the anger over what had been done to Arthur would come crashing out.

Martha said, "I've got time to convince you. I know this cancer won't kill me. God told me."

✢ ✢ ✢

The house was quiet except for the spluttering of the coffee machine. Lane was on the phone a little after seven-thirty. Loraine was an old friend and a child psychologist hired by the police in cases like this where a minor witnessed a crime.

"Hello." Loraine sounded like she was sipping a drink.

"It's Lane," he said.

"I'm going to phone around eight o'clock and arrange a time with Jay and Cole. Do you want to be there?" she asked.

"It's not a problem?" Lane wondered how Cole would respond to having a detective there.

Loraine read his mind. "You're a familiar face. He may trust you. I need you there."

Lane said, "Call me with a time, please. Is Lisa there?"

"Just a minute. It's for you, honey." Loraine set the phone down.

Lisa picked it up. "Lane?"

"I've got a question about the Reddie crime scene," Lane said.

"I hear you found the car," Lisa said.

"Yes. Finally, a break. About the campsite. Were you able to find any footprints?" Lane asked.

"A couple of partials. Bobbie and Charles had similar shoe sizes. The partials were indistinct, but I do have photographs. What have you got?" Lisa asked.

"Footprints from a crime scene in Jamaica. Three deaths at a resort. It's confirmed that Bobbie was there at the time," Lane said.

"Can you send me copies?" Lisa asked.

"Yes. Why?" Lane asked.

"We've got a guy working on footprinting. He's good. He might be able to tell you more than you'd thought possible."

"Are we talking smoking gun?" Lane asked.

"Perhaps," Lisa said.

"When they arrive, I'll get Harper to send a copy your way. Thanks, Lisa," he said.

"Lane?"

"Yes," Lane said.

"If you're right, you've got at least five deaths attributed to this individual. I'd be very careful," Lisa said.

"It may be as many as seven," Lane said.

"All the more reason to be careful," Lisa said.

Lane's next call was to Harper.

"Hello, Lane," Harper said.

"You're psychic," Lane said.

"Caller ID. Old technology," Harper said.

"When the footprints come in, make copies and send them to Lisa. You've got her number?" Lane said.

"Yep. You goin' to see the kid?" Harper asked.

"You need to be there too. We need a recording," Lane said.

"I'm on it. What time?"

"Be ready and I'll call you," Lane said.

"Right." Harper hung up.

The phone rang before Lane could call to see if Jay and Cole were up.

"Hello?" Lane said.

Chief said, "It's me."

"Good morning," Lane said.

"Bring me up to speed."

"The car, which may have transported Kaylie Reddie's body to the crime scene, is being analyzed now. We may be able to prove that its contents have been undisturbed. Footprints from the Jamaica crime scene are set to arrive today and copies will be sent for RCMP analysis. A psychologist is standing by to interview Cole Reddie. Some of the evidence might offer a plausible explanation for the anomalies at the crime scene. So, we have the potential for a strong case against Bobbie Reddie," Lane said.

Chief's anger was barely under control. "Unfortunately, we can't take *potential* to court. We may need to have overwhelming proof. Did you hear Ms. Reddie's radio show yesterday?"

"No," Lane said.

"She is doing her best to create a public uproar over her son being in police custody. I've got a press conference in two hours," she said.

"We need Bobbie to provide copies of her footprints," Lane said.

Chief asked, "How many murders might be attributed to Ms. Reddie?"

"Seven," Lane said.

"Go through it again for me," she said.

"Bobbie's parents, the three victims in Jamaica, Kaylie and Charles Reddie," Lane said.

"That's it?"

"Yes," Lane said.

Chief asked, "The footprints will tie Ms. Reddie to three deaths?"

"Perhaps as many as five. There are partial footprints from the Charles and Kaylie Reddie crime scene," Lane said.

"Good. I'll request that Ms. Reddie voluntarily present herself for footprinting in order to eliminate herself in the investigation of the three deaths in Jamaica," she said.

"Taking the offensive?" Lane asked.

"I think it's time. We've been taking it from Ms. Reddie. Now it's our turn. There is a problem, however."

"What's that?" Lane asked.

"If you are correct in your suspicions, then we may be pushing a multiple murderer into a corner," she said.

"So far, her reactions have been very predictable," Lane said.

"What do you mean?"

"She either bullies, manipulates or plays the victim," Lane said.

Chief said, "You're forgetting that she kills."

"No, I'm not," Lane said.

"Good, because we have a reliable source who disclosed that Ms. Reddie knows where you live. Bobbie was tipped by a caller and a guest. Our source made a point of warning me to watch out for you."

"What else do you know?" Lane asked.

"That I've never experienced more pressure than I have with this case. The more pressure we get, the more I'm convinced you're on to something."

"We'll keep on it," Lane said.

"And you'll listen to the news conference?"

"I will," Lane said.

+ + +

"So, where are the footprints?" Lane asked.

They sat in their Chevy outside the condominium where Jay and Cole were staying. The complex was located close to the river. Across the water, the banks rose to a bluff. Douglas firs grew up the steep bank helping to keep it stabilized and green year-round.

"As soon as it arrives at the station, we get a call," Harper said. "It's on the way."

"Loraine's been inside at least an hour," Lane said.

Harper sipped his coffee. "At least the coffee's good. Since I partnered with you, I haven't had a bad cup of coffee. Are you all ready for Halloween?"

"Halloween?" Lane asked.

"Don't tell me." Harper looked at Lane like he had forgotten to put on a pair of pants.

"It's tomorrow night?" The look on Lane's face told Harper all he needed to know.

"Arthur's got it covered, right?"

"I sure hope so," Lane said.

"Probably won't be too many kids. That storm is supposed to hit by noon. They're forecasting fifteen to twenty centimetres of snow," Harper said.

The phone rang.

Lane said, "Hello." He nodded at Harper. "We're on our way up."

Five minutes later, when they stepped inside the living room, both boys were watching TV. Jay waved. Cole was transfixed by what he saw on the screen. He sat with legs crossed and back straight.

Loraine sat at the kitchen table. She was dressed in neutral colours; greys and browns. Next to her was an officer dressed in street blues. Harper sat down across from the officer and said, "Harper."

"Andrea." She shook hands with Harper.

"We're waiting for the news conference," Loraine said.

"The kid insisted," Andrea said.

"Jay?" Harper asked.

"No, it was Cole," Loraine said.

Lane watched the child. Cole didn't move and blinked only occasionally.

They waited that way for more than ten minutes.

Jay shifted his weight a few times.

Cole blinked.

"This is a v Channel news special," the announcer said.

Every eye in the room focused on the television.

"The Calgary Chief of Police has called a news conference to explain the decision to place Cole Reddie, son of Bobbie Reddie, in protective custody. We are live."

Chief Wyatt stood behind a cluster of microphones. She stood erect and stared back at the camera.

"It's time to release the facts. The tragic deaths of Kaylie and Charles Reddie have resulted in an extremely complex and difficult investigation. Police practices and procedures require that we be as thorough and cautious as possible with this type of crime.

"A number of facts have been uncovered to this point. Kaylie Reddie died of Shaken Baby Syndrome and was dead at least twelve hours before her father. Charles Reddie died from an allergic reaction to penicillin. More recent evidence has come to light and is in the process of being evaluated.

"Both Jay Krocker, Ms. Reddie's brother, and Cole Reddie, Ms. Reddie's son, are under protective custody. Since Cole Reddie is a minor, this is as much information as the police department is able to share even though Jay and Cole's pictures have already been released through the media. It must be made clear to the public that Jay and Cole are being held for their own protection.

"In a related matter, Bobbie Reddie's lawyer has been contacted. I am requesting that Ms. Reddie submit to a footprinting in order to eliminate her as a suspect in a separate murder investigation. Further details related to the case will be released at a later date. Thank you."

Chief Wyatt turned away from the microphones, and the camera shifted to a V Channel news reporter.

Jay reached up and switched the television off.

Cole stared at the blank screen.

Harper said, "That's sure gonna get people talking."

"Mommy said there'd be a fire if I said anything," Cole said.

Loraine stood up and waved Lane closer. Then Loraine looked at Harper and Andrea. The glare gave a clear message—leave the room.

Harper went to set his tape recorder on the coffee table.

Loraine shook her head to say no.

Andrea and Harper left the room.

"Cole?" Loraine waited until the child looked at

her. “We need to talk. Where would you like to sit?”

“By the window.” Cole walked toward the easy chair near the window and sat.

Lane and Loraine sat on the couch while Jay grabbed a chair from the kitchen and completed a lop-sided circle.

Loraine leaned forward.

Cole watched her warily.

“We would like to ask you some questions,” Loraine said.

“You want to know what happened to Kaylie and my dad,” Cole said.

“Cole’s smart. You have to talk with him like he’s an adult,” Jay said.

Loraine said, “You’re right Cole, that’s what we want to know. Are you able to tell us anything about what happened to your sister or father?”

“Kaylie wanted to go and see my dad. She said she was going to ride her bike to see him,” Cole said.

Lane remembered the pink bicycle sitting in the Reddie front yard.

“What happened then?” Loraine asked.

“My mom took the wheel off of Kaylie’s bike.” Cole stared out the window, reliving the experience.

Loraine waited.

Lane saw tears running down the boy’s cheeks. Cole wiped them away with a sleeve. “I thought my mom and Kaylie were asleep, so I took Eddie to the vet.”

“Eddie?” Loraine asked.

“The dog,” Lane said.

"Can you tell us more about Eddie?" Loraine asked.

"His ear was cut off, and his paw was hurt. He was bleeding," Cole said.

"Do you know what happened to Eddie?" Loraine asked.

"Yes, Kaylie made my mom mad." Cole wiped his eyes.

"I don't understand," Loraine said.

"Kaylie was bad, so Eddie's foot was smashed with a hammer. Kaylie still wanted to see my dad, so Eddie lost an ear." Cole's voice was beginning to sound disconnected from the experience.

Loraine waited, formulating a careful question. "Will you tell us more?"

"Punishments and reward." Cole took a long shuddering breath. "If we were bad, my mom would hurt Eddie. If we were good, she would take Eddie to the vet."

Loraine looked away, shook her head, then took a breath.

Lane thought, So *far, everything he's said is supported by the vet, Dr. Dent.*

"Will you tell us more about that night?" Loraine asked.

"I came home. The lights were on. My mom said I had to get in the car," Cole said.

"Is there more?" Loraine asked.

"Yes." Cole began to sob. Tears and mucous created a sheen on his cheeks, lips, and chin.

Loraine waited.

"Will the footprints match?" Cole asked.

Lane said, "We don't know yet." *This kid has really thought this through,* Lane decided. He looked at Jay.

"When will you know?" Cole asked.

"It depends on how hard it is for us to get a footprint from Bobbie Reddie," Lane said.

"It's hot in Jamaica. People don't wear shoes there do they?" Cole asked.

Lane looked at Jay.

Jay shrugged as if to say, 'I told you.'

"My mom said if I say anything about what happened to my sister or my dad, then someone will burn," Cole said.

"Are you afraid she'll burn you?" Loraine asked.

Cole's voice was as hollow as a house that hasn't been lived in for a month when he said, "That's not how it works."

Loraine spent a half-hour more talking with Cole. No more information was forthcoming except when Cole said, "If the footprint does match, then ask. Kaylie is dead. My dad is dead. I don't want anyone else to be dead."

Lane said, "Eddie isn't dead. You saved Eddie."

Cole looked back with an unfamiliar expression. An emotion that, up to this point, had been out of place on the child's face. It took till the evening for Lane to understand that he had seen hope in Cole's eyes.

+ + +

"Matt wants to hand out candy to the kids tomorrow night," Arthur said. They stood together at the arena.

Martha wore a blue satin scarf to keep her head warm and stood next to her brother. Lane had a few minutes before he had to get changed.

"I forgot all about Halloween," Lane said.

"I'd be happier if everyone forgot about Halloween. It's not very Christian," Martha said.

"You've really had your nose deep in this case," Arthur said to Lane as if he hadn't heard his sister.

"I still do," Lane said.

"You're worried about the kid," Arthur said.

"If we don't solve this one soon, the boy could go back home," Lane said.

"Over my dead body! There's no way on God's green earth that Matt's going back to his father!" Martha said.

"We're not talking about Matt," Arthur said.

"Oh," Martha said.

"Hey! Lane! How you doin'?"

They turned to face Bob, the head referee. He had a big smile on his Marine recruiting poster face and a brand new haircut.

"I'm Bob." He held out his hand to Arthur. "Nice shiners."

"I'm Arthur and this is my sister, Martha," Arthur said.

"Nice scarf," Bob said to Martha before turning to Lane. "Heard you've had some fan problems lately and you handled 'em. We're getting calls from people who say they like your work. Never happened before. Then there's the asshole, Mac, who called to complain that he got arrested. But, then everybody in hockey knows he's an asshole!" Bob slapped Arthur on the back.

Arthur's eyes reflected a mixture of amusement and shock.

"We'd better get changed," Lane said.

"Don't worry, Arthur. I'll keep Lane safe!" Bob winked at Martha.

Lane thought, *It's going to be a long night.*

Bob talked all the way down the hall, during the time it took to change, and while he skated behind Lane as they circled the ice. Bob just wouldn't shut up.

"We're buddies," Bob said several times.

Lane decided there was a hell, and maybe Martha was right afterall. *If Bob didn't shut up,* Lane decided, *he was either going to have to find religion, or dismember the head referee.*

Bob didn't let up through the first fifty-nine minutes of the game. "Amazing, simply amazing. That nephew of yours is amazing. Sure knows how to protect a one-goal lead. Only a minute left, and he's keepin' his team in the game. Listen to the crowd." The parents were chanting while the teams changed lines for perhaps the last time. The face-off was in the opposing end.

The centres cruised over and took their positions. Lane stood between them. He looked around to make sure the wingers and defencemen were properly aligned.

"OFFENCE!" the parents at one end of the stands roared.

"DEFENCE!" the parents at Arthur and Martha's end roared.

Lane dropped the puck.

The centre poked the puck between the legs of Matt's centre.

Matt's defencemen turned to intercept the opposing centre, who accelerated down the ice. The centre squirted between the defencemen. There was nothing but open ice between him and Matt.

"BREAKAWAY!" a fan yelled.

Lane skated down the left side, a stride behind the centre. He glanced down the ice. Matt had his goalie stick hitched up awkwardly in his right hand. His glove hand opened and closed.

The centre deeked right and went left.

Matt tried to follow. He lost and regained his balance.

The centre shot high for the open top-half of the net.

Matt's glove hand rose up. His elbow worked like a cog with a few teeth missing. The glove jerked up.

The centre raised his hands, certain the puck was going in.

Matt's glove plucked the puck out of the air.

The crowd roared.

Bob blew his whistle and waved his arms to indicate no goal.

Matt fell over.

Lane leaned over to take the puck from Matt's glove.

"Nice save," Lane said.

"Thanks, Uncle." Matt's invisible grin seemed to stretch the width of his face mask.

They drove home with the windows open. Lane and Matt were sitting in the back seat. Lane was sure he smelled better than Matt who smiled, elbowed Lane, and said, "Uncle, you stink."

Lane felt a momentary, unfamiliar glow of acceptance. He found himself grinning all the way home.

Saturday, October 31

Chapter 23

TONY REACHED FOR the phone. His voice was thick with sleep when he said, "Hello?"

"It's me," Jay said.

"You okay, man?" Tony asked.

"Yep," Jay said.

"Cole okay?" Tony asked.

"He finally fell asleep. Figure I've got a little bit of time before the nightmares start," Jay said.

"Man, what time is it?" Tony covered his eyes as his mother opened his bedroom door and turned on the light. He put the receiver on his shoulder and said, "It's okay, mom, it's Jay."

She frowned and closed the door, leaving the light on.

Jay said, "It's three o'clock. Look, I need Rosie's number."

"Man, you're crazy if you call her now, she'll—"

"I need to talk with her," Jay said.

"If I give you the number, will you wait seven hours? I mean she's really grumpy in the morning."

"Okay," Jay said.

Tony gave him the number.

"Thanks," Jay said.

Tony said, "You and Cole are all over the news. My mom watches it all the time. You're a star."

"Tell me about it. Cole's like a zombie sitting in

front of the TV. If we shut off the TV, it's worse. Then, he does this nonstop talking routine. It's scary. We can't get outta here. It's drivin' me crazy," Jay said.

"At least Bobbie can't get at you there."

Jay laughed. "We're prisoners and she's free. Go figure. Shit!" Jay said.

"What's the matter, man?" Tony heard the wail of a child in pain.

"Kaylie!" Cole said. "Why can't Kaylie ride up here with me?"

"Gotta go, man. Cole's havin' a nightmare." Jay hung up.

Jay made it to Cole's room about three steps ahead of the police officer, Andrea.

"Kaylie!" Cole said.

Cole's voice crawled up Jay's spine and sparked a memory. The image of his parents, and their closed coffins. His sister crying and smiling at him behind her handkerchief. A smile only Jay was meant to see.

Jay lifted Cole to a sitting position. The back of the child's T-shirt was wet with perspiration. "Cole, it's me, Jay."

"Uncle Jay?" Cole asked without opening his eyes.

"It's me, Cole. I'm here," Jay said.

Cole opened one eye, blinking at the light. "Kaylie?"

"She died, Cole," Jay said.

Cole sobbed, shivered, and wept for a solid half-hour until falling asleep.

Andrea sat there, waiting, without saying a word.

Jay covered Cole.

"You need some sleep?" Andrea asked.

"Maybe later." Cole's nightmare had left Jay wide awake and energized by an adrenaline rush.

Andrea sat down in the front-room chair and swivelled it so she could face Jay. "Loraine said she'd be here again in the morning."

"Can we call her when Cole gets up? He might sleep for a while now," Jay said.

"I'll ask."

"I'm gonna make a phone call." Jay stood up.

Andrea said, "Absolutely no clues about where we are. And I mean absolutely none."

"Deal." Jay sat down at the kitchen table before reaching for the phone on the wall.

The phone rang ten times at the other end before a voice mumbled, "Hello?"

"Rosie?" Jay said.

"Who's this?"

"Jay. I'm sorry, Rosie, but . . ." Jay said.

The words at the other end came in a rush of Vietnamese.

Jay didn't understand the words, but he got the message. "Look, it's the only time I could call. I'm sorry but I wanted to talk with you."

"How's Cole?" Rosie's tone said all was not forgiven, yet.

"Asleep," Jay said.

"More nightmares?" Rosie asked.

"And he's beginning to cry. I think he's grieving. Or

maybe it's safe to cry now. I don't know. The front of my T-shirt is soaked."

"Spilling more than you're eating?" Rosie began to chuckle.

"Does this mean I'm forgiven?"

"Not yet, but keep talking," Rosie said.

+ + +

Lane awoke to the sound of someone with the dry heaves.

Arthur breathed deeply next to him.

"I swear, you could sleep through an earthquake," Lane said. The reply was more snoring.

Lane got up and looked in the open door of the bathroom. Martha was on her knees at the toilet, wiping her mouth with a tissue.

"Want some water?" Lane asked.

She slowly turned to look at him over her left shoulder and nodded.

Lane went into the kitchen. Riley nudged him with his nose as Lane filled a glass with water. He patted the dog's flank. Riley ambled into the dining room and settled under the table.

"Thanks," Martha said as Lane handed her the glass. She sat on the closed toilet lid and sipped tentatively.

"Feeling any better?" Lane asked.

"A little bit." Martha looked directly at Lane. "You'll take care of Matt for me. You and Arthur, you'd do that for me?"

"Yes," Lane said.

"Good." She nodded, stood, and grabbed the towel railing.

"Going back to bed?" Lane asked.

"Nope. I want to see the sunrise." She pulled out what appeared to be a cigarette from her housecoat pocket. "And I'm smoking this while I watch." Martha held the joint up so Lane could see it.

"Where'd you get that?" Lane thought, *What am I going to do, arrest her?*

"A guy at the hospital gave me a couple. Said that it would help if the nausea got rough. Got any matches?"

"I think Arthur keeps some wooden ones in the kitchen for lighting candles." Lane thought, *I hope this helps, because you must have lost another five kilos.*

Five minutes later, they sat wrapped in their winter coats in the backyard. The pungent smell of weed filled the air while pinks, oranges, and purples filled the sky. "The air is cold this morning," Martha said.

"We're supposed to get a snowstorm later today."

"Feels like something's coming our way." Martha took another tentative puff of weed.

+ + +

"What's that smell?" Harper asked.

"What smell?" Lane said.

They sat next to the window in a coffee shop on Parkdale Boulevard, about four blocks away from the place where Jay and Cole were staying. It was in-between lunch and dinner. A group of four people sat at the other end of the shop.

"Weed, Lane. Weed. You smell like weed," Harper said.

"Martha's smoking it to help with the nausea from the chemo."

"Oh, shit. I'm sorry." Harper began to laugh.

Lane chuckled, "Thought you had me, eh officer?"

"Glad you still have a sense of humour," Harper said.

"So am I." *And I'd like about twenty-four hours of nightmare-free sleep,* Lane thought.

Harper decided to get down to business. "Lisa has a copy of the footprint from Jamaica. She's getting her expert to take a look. We haven't heard anything back from Bobbie's lawyer. Might not hear till next week. Dr. Fibre is still working on the samples from the trunk of Bobbie's Chrysler. The newspapers are full of stories about Bobbie Reddie, and how she thinks the police are victimizing her. So far, only one editorial says Bobbie should provide the footprint. After all, she's got nothing to hide."

"Chief got anything new to say?" Lane asked.

"Not this morning."

Lane looked outside. A car pulled up in front of the coffee shop. The driver stepped out. The wind whipped at his hair and swung his door open. The white fog of the driver's breath appeared and was carried south. A few snowflakes plastered themselves against the glass in front of Lane.

They waited, rehashing the case, and keeping an eye

on the weather. The call came at about three o'clock.

Lane's phone rang. He flipped it open.

"It's Loraine," she said.

"I'm sitting here drinking coffee with Harper," Lane said.

"Call it a day. Cole is still asleep. Apparently, he had another bad dream last night. He cried himself out. A good thing, I hope. Anyway, Jay and I are getting to know one another. You know, he's been on his own since he was fifteen? He managed to graduate high school, and now he's working on a degree in psychology. It's beginning to look like he's had lots of first hand experience dealing with abhorrent behaviour. Anyway, I'm heading home as soon as the next officer arrives to relieve Andrea," Loraine said.

"Say hello to Lisa for us," Lane said.

"Oh, I almost forgot, she sent the footprint and the impression from the Jamaican crime scene to the expert. She asked me to pass that on," Loraine said.

"Thanks. We'll see you tomorrow?" Lane asked.

"Maybe tomorrow we'll be able to talk with Cole." Loraine hung up.

✢ ✢ ✢

Riley was waiting with his leash in his mouth when Lane walked in the door. There was a hint of marijuana in the air.

Arthur asked, "How are the roads?"

"Getting slippery. Give it a few more hours, and it'll be tricky. Glad I'm not a traffic cop," Lane said.

"Don't worry about Riley, Matt just took him for a long walk. Supper's in half an hour. The trick-or-treaters should be at the door soon."

Riley huffed, turned his back, and sat sulking under the dining-room table.

"I'm going to have a quick nap on the couch." Lane sat down. *Just twenty minutes,* Lane thought.

Riley barked.

Lane opened an eye. He looked at his watch, realizing he had been asleep for more than an hour.

"Trick or treat!"

Lane swung his legs around and sat up. He tucked his feet into his slippers. Shaking his head, he got up and made for the front door.

Two tots in dog costumes held pillowcases open, while Matt dropped miniature chocolates inside. "Thanks!" the kids said and ran down the stairs. One skidded, nearly fell, and righted himself.

Riley cocked his head to one side.

"Never seen dogs like that before, have you, Riley?" Matt rubbed the dog's head. Riley closed his eyes, savouring the moment.

The doorbell rang. Lane turned. Riley barked. Matt opened the door.

Mrs. Smallway stood there with a bag in her hand. She shivered on the top step. The wind whipped at the black silk kimono she wore. "I'm having some friends over." She used her free hand to keep the front of her kimono closed.

"That's nice," Matt said.

Lane couldn't think of one thing to say. He noticed Mrs. Smallway had done her makeup. She reminded him of a television-evangelist's wife, despite the geisha lipstick. The blizzard could not move one hair in her beehive hairdo. Lane decided that someone might see a certain innocence in her expression, but he knew her better than that.

"Here are my Halloween candies. Tell the kids not to ring my doorbell." Smallway handed the bag to Matt, turning her back, and walked away.

Matt let the door close. "There sure are some strange people living in this city."

Lane, still at a loss for words, took the bag from Matt, and set it down around the corner. He thought of at least a dozen things to say before deciding on, "Where's everybody?"

"Uncle Arthur's taking a nap and Mom's asleep," Matt said. Riley licked his hand. "The storm's really gettin' bad." He pointed at the full-length safety glass in the screen door. Frost coated the bottom half.

"Any coffee made?" Lane tried not to think too much about the motives behind Mrs. Smallway's request.

"Think Uncle Arthur made a pot," Matt said.

Lane went to investigate and heard Matt turn the TV on.

Lane filled two cups, then put his winter boots on. He pulled on a jacket and stepped outside. The wind whipped snow into his face. He made his way across the street where the unmarked police car sat idling. The driver opened her window. He handed her one cup and another to the passenger. "Thanks. I'm Amanda." She offered her free hand.

"Lane." He shook her hand.

"Frank." The other officer reached across to shake Lane's hand.

"Let me know if you need anything." Lane spotted a photo of Bobbie Reddie sitting on the seat cushion.

"We will." The corners of Amanda's mouth wrinkled when she smiled. Her hair was red and cut short. Frank's hair was cut so short, it was hard to see if he usually had any, let alone what colour it might be.

Lane heard a car door shut and looked to his left. A bull got out of a car parked in front of Mrs. Smallway's house. At least the head was a bull, the rest walked like a man dressed in black.

"He's number four," Amanda said.

"Looks like the wild kingdom lives next door to you. First a white stallion then an elephant. The last one was a unicorn. Got a zookeeper next door?" Frank asked.

"Something like that. I'll put on a fresh pot." While Lane crossed the street, he thought about Mrs. Smallway's glassed-in addition and what Matt might see if he looked out his bedroom window. Lane stepped over a drift running across his sidewalk and opened the front door.

The TV was on but Riley and Matt were gone. Lane heard a voice in the back bedroom. He took off his boots, put on his slippers, and went down the hall. He peeked in the door. Arthur and Matt stood on the bed, pressing their faces against the window.

"Maybe we'd better not look," Arthur said.

"That's gross!" Matt said.

"I'd have to agree with you there," Arthur said.

"What's up?" Lane asked.

Matt and Arthur turned. They looked at Lane, then at each other. Matt started to laugh.

"Actually, that's a good question." Arthur stepped off the bed. Matt followed.

"Some kind of party." Matt moved past Lane.

"That's right. A social gathering," Arthur said.

"Not much doubt what they're doin'," Matt began to laugh again. His runners squeaked as he went down the hall.

"Not much doubt at all," Arthur said.

Riley followed Lane down the hall and into the kitchen.

"New shoes?" Lane asked.

"Yep," Matt said.

Lane said, "I'd better make a fresh pot of coffee."

He followed Arthur, who sat down at the kitchen table.

Matt squeaked all the way to the front door to see if any more trick-or-treaters were arriving.

Riley went to the dining room and curled up under the table next to the window.

+ + +

Amanda sipped her coffee. "Not bad."

"What's this?" Frank nodded at the black Acura parking around the corner in front of Lane's driveway.

A person dressed in black stepped out of the car.

"The ninja outfit will fit right in at the neighbour's party," Frank said.

The ninja went to the back of the Acura and opened the trunk.

"It's a woman," Amanda said.

"How can you tell?" Frank asked.

"I just can."

The woman stepped from behind the trunk. In her right hand she carried a bottle with a flaming wick. She put another bottle in her jacket pocket and a third in her left hand.

"Shit. Molotov cocktails!" Frank spilled coffee in his lap when he reached to open his door.

Bobbie walked closer to the dining-room window. She touched the flaming wick to the bottle in her left hand. With an underhand toss, she threw one bottle through the window.

Riley was startled by the sound of shattered glass. He stood, then darted from under the protection of the table. The retriever's back was showered with glass, gasoline, and flame.

Lane turned as the glass broke. He heard Riley howl.

Arthur stood.

The dog was a fireball. Riley hit Arthur behind the

knees. Arthur's head caught the edge of the table as he fell to the floor. Riley careened down the hall, then launched himself through the glass of the front door. The safety glass exploded into pebble-sized bits.

"Riley!" Matt jumped through the empty aluminum door frame and ran out into the storm.

Flames spilled onto the floor. The dining room filled with black smoke. The air was tainted with the stench of gasoline.

Lane ran down the hall and opened Martha's door. He threw her blanket back, pulling her to her feet.

"Wha . . . ?" she asked.

"Move!" Lane pushed her toward the door.

"My head's spinning," Martha said.

Lane tucked his head under her arm and half-carried her down the hall. He saw Arthur on the floor. "Arthur! Jesus! Arthur, get up!" Smoke and flame filled the dining and living rooms as he turned right, stepping over the broken glass.

"My feet!" Glass ripped the soles of Martha's feet.

Lane heard two gunshots.

+ + +

"Stay still!" Frank ordered. He pulled his Glock from its holster and pointed it at Bobbie. Wind-driven snow obscured his vision.

Bobbie looked directly at Frank, pulled another bottle from a jacket pocket, touched it to the lit wick, then stood with her arms extended.

"Stay still!" Amanda stood about five metres to the

right of Frank. Her Glock was ready.

Bobbie tossed one bottle at Frank's feet. The glass shattered. Liquid fire poured over his shoes and licked up his pant legs.

"Oh, Jesus!" Frank jumped left into a snow drift.

Bobbie cocked her arm to throw the remaining cocktail at Amanda.

Amanda fired twice. Both rounds hit Bobbie in the chest. Bobbie looked down at the front of her jacket. She sat down in slow motion, then leaned to the right. The cocktail in her hand tilted. The wick ignited the gasoline. It glowed under the snow as it ran down into the gutter.

Bobbie looked at Amanda and said, "How could you shoot me?" Bobbie stared at the bottle and reached for it.

Amanda kicked the bottle away from Bobbie.

+ + +

Lane sat Martha down on the sidewalk. He looked up the street. Through the blowing snow, he spotted Riley. The dog was a yellow flame disappearing around the corner.

"Riley!" Matt's voice carried on the wind.

Martha said, "Arthur! Where's Arthur?"

Lane looked at the house. It glowed from the inside. Smoke was beginning to billow out the top of the broken front door.

Lane followed Martha's bloody footsteps back into the house. He stepped through the aluminum frame.

Inside, he dropped to his knees. The smoke was just above his head. He crawled into the kitchen. He looked into the dining room. Oxygen was being sucked in through the broken windows. He found Arthur in the kitchen. Lane grabbed Arthur's shirt-collar and dragged him down the hall.

Lane coughed. The smoke grew thicker. The hair on his head and arms felt as if it might burst into flame.

Still on his hands and knees, Lane backed out the front door, lifted Arthur under the arms, and hauled him down the stairs.

Someone grabbed Arthur's feet.

It was the police officer, Amanda. She said, "Get him in the car! I've called for help. Anybody else inside?"

"No," Lane said.

They carried Arthur to the car. Martha was already inside. Lane caught a whiff of burned flesh. Frank sat in the front seat and moaned.

"Help's coming Frank! Hold on!" Amanda said.

"Arthur?" Martha asked.

They propped Arthur in the back seat. He leaned up against his sister. There was a bump the size of a plum on the side of his head.

Lane and Amanda looked at Bobbie lying on the sidewalk. Both opened their doors. Amanda went to the trunk and pulled out a blanket. Lane picked up the first aid kit. They walked across the street.

Bobbie was on her side. She looked at Amanda. "She shot me! I was unarmed and she shot me." The voice was cotton candy sweet.

Amanda leaned and put the blanket over Bobbie's feet. Then the officer pressed her hands against the wounds to slow the blood loss.

Lane opened the first-aid kit.

Bobbie said, "I'm going to destroy both of you!"

Lane looked at Bobbie.

She was staring at him. "I know everything about you, you pervert. How's your boyfriend? He's still inside isn't he? Serves him right!"

Bobbie turned to Amanda. "And you, you bitch, you shot me for nothing! Once I get back on the radio, you're going to have to crawl into a hole! I'll destroy you!"

Lane looked at Amanda. There were tears running down her cheeks.

Lane pulled out two sterile bandages. He ripped open the packages. The wind whipped the wrappings away. Amanda's sobs reached him. He looked at Amanda, then to Bobbie whose mouth was open. Her eyes were unfocused and staring into the storm.

"Amanda?" Lane said.

She looked back at him.

"We think Bobbie killed seven people. One was a child."

"I think her heart stopped." Amanda lifted her bloody gloves away from the body. She checked for a pulse.

"She's gone. Let's get back to the blue and white." He walked beside her back to the car. She got into the driver's seat.

"Where's Matt?" Martha asked.

Lane leaned on the open passenger door. "I'll go get him."

"What happened to you?" Martha asked.

Lane looked at his hands. They were bleeding. Blood dripped and was carried downwind where it spattered the fresh snow. He looked at his knees. His pants were soaked with blood. "Glass." Lane wondered why there was no pain.

"Where's my Matt?" Martha began to scream. "Matt!"

Lane said, "Martha! He's all right. He went after Riley."

Lane looked at the house. It was fully engulfed now. Flame rolled out the front door. All of the windows were glowing. The snow on the roof was turning to steam.

To the right of the house, on the sidewalk, there was the glow of flame from the Molotov cocktail next to Bobbie's body.

Lane could hear the sirens now. He pulled down the sleeves of his shirt so he could grip the cuffs in his palms and slow the blood flow. The wind-driven pellets of snow stung Lane's face. He prayed that Matt had managed to find Riley and put out the fire. He walked past Mrs. Smallway's house.

The front door opened. Mrs. Smallway was wearing a different kimono. "Is a little privacy too much to ask for?"

Lane looked at his house, then back at his neighbour. "You'd better get out!" He pointed at the flames.

Mrs. Smallway's mouth opened and closed. She stepped outside to get a better look.

He turned into the wind and walked north. His ears were beginning to freeze. His toes were numb. He found Matt and Riley two blocks away in a neighbour's front yard. Riley had dropped into the snow next to a parked car. Snow was covering his blackened fur and flesh.

"Riley must have been blinded by the fire, because he ran right into the side of the car. He hasn't moved since," Matt said.

Riley's fur had been burned to the skin. Lane saw that his ribs weren't moving.

The wind shifted. Lane inhaled the stench of burned hair and flesh.

Matt began to weep.

Lane put his hand at the back of Matt's neck. Then, remembering his wounds, pulled way, leaving a bloody hand-print on the back of Matt's shirt. Snow coated Matt's hair.

Matt patted Riley's nose, then tried the dog's paw, hoping for some kind of response.

"Matt, he's dead."

Matt's head dropped.

Lane clenched his hands against the pain. "We have to get back, Matt."

They left Riley where he'd fallen and walked back to the fire.

When Matt and Lane reached the house, the street

was blocked with fire trucks, police cars, ambulances, a rescue truck, and reporters.

"Look at that!" Matt said.

Mrs. Smallway's house was burning. She stood across the street in her borrowed kimono. Four men stood beside her. They wore kimonos and animal masks. A reporter aimed his camera. Its light pushed back the darkness to shine on Smallway and her escorts. "Piss off!" Mrs. Smallway said.

A gust of wind blew the kimonos open. The four men stood at attention. The camera panned from left to right capturing the image of the four in masks; a horse, elephant, unicorn and bull with their erect, out-of-season Maypoles blown sideways by a gust of wind. The four members were quickly covered up when Mrs. Smallway said, "Christ you guys! Use your manners!"

A reporter turned to the woman with the camera and asked, "Did you get that?"

Lane and Matt walked past. Only the far wall of Lane and Arthur's house stood. Firemen aimed their hoses at Mrs. Smallway's house. Smoke rolled under the edges of her roof, before curling up to be carried away by the storm. The night was filled with the sound of diesel engines running water pumps. Blue and red lights reflected off the snow. Lane stared at the *Go Flames Go!* poster in the window of one fire truck.

"Hey, Lane!" a police officer said. "We've been lookin' for you! Get yourself looked after!"

Two officers in blue nylon jackets grabbed him by

the elbows. They guided him to the back of one of the ambulances.

An officer said, "You! We've got another injured cop here. Move!"

A paramedic opened the back door of the ambulance. Lane was heaved up and in through the back door. The paramedic sat him down.

"Where's everyone else?" Lane asked.

"The policeman with the burns is on the way to the hospital. Some guy and his sister are in another ambulance. They just left for the hospital. The one on the ground was pronounced dead at the scene."

One of the officers poked his head in the back of the ambulance. Lane said, "See the body over there? Disturb the scene as little as possible. Did you check her?"

The officer looked over his shoulder and spotted the yellow blanket coated with snow. "She took two in the chest. She's dead. The paramedics checked her out too."

"The crime scene needs to be taped off. Double-check to make sure the fire's out. We need her footprints," Lane said.

"Footprints?" the officer asked.

"That's correct," Lane said.

"Okay." The officer left.

"I need a phone, please," Lane said.

"Got one up front," the paramedic said.

Matt pulled himself into the back of the ambulance. The door closed behind him.

The paramedic examined Lane's hands. "Looks like you'll need stitches." He tore the wrapping off a packet of bandages.

"Where's the phone?" Lane asked.

"Here." The driver passed the phone back.

"Matt, take it." Lane told Matt the number.

"Okay." Matt dialed and put it to Lane's ear.

"Hello?" Harper said.

"It's Lane. I need a favour. Riley's dead. I need someone to pick up the body."

"Where?" Harper asked.

Lane looked at the paramedic, "Where are we going?"

"Foothills."

"Can you pick Matt up at the Foothills Hospital? He'll show you where." Lane handed the phone back to the driver. "We can leave as soon as the Forensic Crime Scenes Unit arrives."

Sunday, November 1

Chapter 24

POLICE GUN DOWN
LOCAL RADIO PERSONALITY

Bobbie Reddie, the star of a popular afternoon radio show, was shot dead last night by police.

Police claim that Reddie threw a firebomb at the home of a police officer. It is believed to be the home of one of the detectives investigating the deaths of Kaylie and Charles Reddie.

The house was destroyed by the fire. Two of its occupants remain in hospital. The other two occupants were taken to hospital and released . . .

Lane stopped reading. He looked out Harper's kitchen window. The snow left a twenty centimetre plateau atop the picnic table. Snow curled over the roof of the garage and hung like a tired dog's tongue. Harper used a snow shovel to attack the metre high drift running along the sidewalk. He threw snow high into the air where the wind snatched it away.

"Uncle read the article this morning, then he went outside to shovel the walk. He's pretty pissed off."

Lane looked over his shoulder at Glenn. Harper's nephew was about six feet tall and had his blond hair styled to accentuate the features of his face. He wore red sweats and a grey T-shirt. Lane said, "Can't say I blame your uncle. It's going to take Amanda a long time to deal with what she had to do. Some officers never recover from a killing. She saved our lives, and her partner's too. There's no mention of that. Or that her partner is in the burn unit and will probably need skin grafts."

"What would have happened if she hadn't shot Bobbie?" Glenn asked.

"At the very least, Arthur would be dead. If Bobbie had been allowed to throw another firebomb into the house, I wouldn't have been able to get to Arthur in time."

"Want some breakfast?"

"Ummm. That would be great," Lane said.

"You're lucky you took me up on the offer, I'm the best cook here," Glenn smiled.

"I heard that! If you weren't such a good cook, and my favorite nephew, I'd be offended." Harper's wife, Erinn came around the corner with one hand atop her belly. She'd cut her red hair short at the start of the pregnancy. "Does that mean I get breakfast too?" She sat down across from Lane. Seeing the newspaper headline, she picked up the paper, folded it and sat it on an empty chair. She looked out the window. "He's going to be busy with that snow shovel for a while. He's furious about the coverage. There's no mention of the fact that Bobbie was tossing Molotov cocktails at people. How are your hands?"

Lane looked at the stitches scattered across his palms and fingers. "Sore."

"And the knees?" Glenn asked.

"The same," Lane said.

"Somebody named Loraine called this morning. She wants you to call her back," Glenn said.

"Glenn, be a dear and hand him the phone." Erinn looked at Lane. "Want us to leave?"

Lane took the phone, placed it on its back on the table and pressed the buttons. "No. Usually Loraine does all of the talking. I just listen." He picked up the phone with his fingertips. It rang three times.

"Hello?" Loraine's familiar voice comforted Lane. He was suddenly glad for old friends and new family.

"It's me," Lane said.

"Cole's up and talking. You want the summary, or do you want to come and hear it for yourself?"

"The summary, for now," Lane said.

"You okay?" Loraine asked.

"I will be," Lane said.

"Arthur okay?"

"He's got a bump on his head and a concussion. We pick him up this afternoon, I think."

"Good. Listen, I'm sorry about Riley," Loraine said.

Lane couldn't reply.

Loraine filled the silence. "We told Cole about his mom's death when he woke up this morning. He started to talk. Apparently, his mother woke him up that night and ordered him to get in the car. When he asked where Kaylie was, Bobbie told him she was in the trunk. His mother drove to the gas station, filled up the car, bought a pack of cigarettes, and filled a thermos with slurpee. He watched her pour amoxil—

you know, penicillin—into the slurpee. They drove out to the campsite. Bobbie made Cole stay in the car while she talked with Charles. Cole watched them at the picnic table. She and Charles drank the slurpee. Cole says his dad got red in the face, then had trouble breathing. Bobbie put on some gloves and helped him into the cab of the truck. Then, she opened the trunk, took Kaylie out, pulled a garbage bag up over his sister's head, and put her in the back of the camper. After that, she taped a hose to the tailpipe of the truck, shoved it through an open window in the cab, and taped it shut. She turned on the truck and went back into the camper. On the way home, she told him what would happen if he said anything to anyone. The kid remembered every detail."

"How's he doing?" Lane asked.

"This is going to take a long time, Lane. The kid appears to be okay, but this kind of experience leaves indelible scars," Loraine said.

"How's Jay?" Lane asked.

"He's not saying much. Just sticks close to Cole and listens," Loraine said.

"Does he know he probably saved Cole's life?" Lane asked.

"I'll tell him you say so. There's another thing . . ."

"What's that?" Lane asked.

"We need you and Harper for a ten o'clock meeting on Tuesday morning. I want you to promise me you'll be there," Loraine said.

Tuesday, November 3

Chapter 24

"ARTHUR'S GOING NUTS," Lane said.

"Something to do with the head injury?" Harper concentrated on keeping them in the ruts on John Laurie Boulevard. The city crews were still catching up after the record-breaking snowstorm. The roads were sanded, snow covered, and slick.

"Maybe. Or he was tired of our old furniture, so he's really happy to be shopping for new. The insurance company's budget has got him grinning. Even Matt's getting into it." Lane looked up the road. Soon they'd see the sign in front of Bobbie's church. He thought about last night's nightmare. Two crucified children.

"And Martha?" Harper asked.

"Still in the hospital. The cancer is spreading." Lane kept his hands palm up to keep from snagging the stitches.

"I don't know what to . . ." Harper said.

"There's not much you can say."

They drove in silence for the next few minutes.

Harper said, "The media has been awfully quiet since those footprints matched up. Then Dr. Fibre came through with a match from the trunk of Bobbie's car. Man, yesterday was full of good news. Chief came out of this smelling like a rose."

The road curved. Bobbie's sign came into view.

It stood tall against a white backdrop of snow. It

said, *The Truth Will Set us Free.*

"Some things never change, I guess," Lane said.

"What's that supposed to mean?" Harper asked.

"Despite overwhelming evidence to the contrary, some people will always believe the lie that was Bobbie Reddie," Lane said.

Harper let the car coast as they neared a red light. The Chevy crabbed sideways when he pressed the brake pedal. "Don't worry, I've got it under control." He guided the vehicle out of its skid. "How's the hotel?"

"Matt likes the waterslide and Arthur likes the food. It'll be okay for a while."

The light turned green. The wheels spun. They crept forward.

"I suppose Arthur's already got a real estate agent," Harper laughed.

"As a matter of fact."

"You're kidding?"

"I told you he was going nuts," Lane said. "I think it helps to keep him and Matt busy."

Harper turned into the mall parking lot. He manouevred around mountains of plowed snow and dodged stranded cars before parking in front of the vet's office.

Loraine, Jay, and Cole were getting out of Loraine's Toyota. Cole looked uncertain, and Jay held his nephew's hand. They stepped through the door. Inside, they found the vet, Dr. Dent, who couldn't suppress a smile.

"Dr. Ellen Dent." Harper smiled.

"Come on in." They followed Dr. Dent into a

waiting room. They crowded around the raised examination table. "I'll be right back." The doctor stepped out the back door.

Loraine smiled at Lane.

Jay said, "It's okay, Cole. It's gonna be okay."

"Where is he?" Cole asked.

A dog barked when it heard Cole's voice.

"Eddie!" Cole said.

The dog skidded around the corner on three legs and a cast. Eddie looked hopefully at five pairs of legs, sniffing each in turn, before stopping in front of Cole. Eddie sat on his back legs to look up at Cole.

The boy leaned over and picked up the dog. Cole buried his face in the dog's fur, grinning when Eddie licked his face.

Lane looked at Loraine who studied him. She shook her head at Lane's apparent lack of reaction to Cole's joy.

Lane thought, *Years of hiding will do that to you.*

Loraine moved next to Lane. "Some day it's all going to spill out. The longer it takes . . ."

"The better it will be?" Lane tried to make a joke and failed. He couldn't forget the sight of Riley's charred body in the snow.

Jay said, "Uncle Tran says all of you have to come for lunch."

+ + +

On the way to the restaurant, Harper was in the driver's seat. He said, "Guess Dr. Dent blew a big hole in your theory."

"What do you mean?" Lane asked.

"Some people do recognize the truth, despite evidence to the contrary." Harper leaned his head back and laughed.

Lane said nothing.

At The Lucky Elephant Restaurant, they found Uncle Tran, Rosie and Tony waiting for them.

Cole kept Eddie tucked inside his jacket. The dog poked his head out when he caught a whiff of food.

Uncle Tran shook hands with all who sat around his table.

Loraine said, "It's a pleasure to meet you. Jay speaks very highly of you."

"My pleasure, also," Uncle Tran said.

Tony picked up Cole. The boy put his arm around Tony's shoulder. "Wanna hang out at the mall after lunch?"

"Sure. Hi Rosie," Cole said.

Rosie touched his cheek with her palm.

When they sat, Cole insisted on being next to her.

Conversation was slow. It picked up after they ordered.

"Uncle, tell them about how you got to Canada," Tony said.

Uncle Tran frowned, then told his tale of leaving Saigon. He finished by saying, "And the elephant I carried onto the aircraft was the same one I carried off."

"What happened to the elephant?" Cole asked.

"It's up there." Uncle Tran pointed to the jade-green elephant with its trunk curled into a U. "And

Mr. Lane? How are your wounds healing?"

"They get a little bit better every day."

The food arrived. Lane spotted a white-gold wedding band with tiny-embedded diamonds on the waiter's finger.

Uncle Tran had been watching Lane. Tran said, "He was married last week."

The waiter set a bowl of satay beef-noodle soup in front of Lane. Exotic spices made his mouth water. He looked up at the jade elephant and remembered the name of the restaurant. Lane looked at the diamond fragments glittering in the waiter's ring. He looked at Uncle Tran whose head was cocked to the right to get a better view of Lane. Uncle Tran smiled. All at once, Lane understood why Uncle Tran was not a Canadian citizen and might never become one. Lane also knew how it would be possible for Uncle Tran to educate and house so many people.

Lane smiled at Uncle Tran.

Cole studied Tran and Lane while his fingers lifted a shrimp from his bowl of noodles and guided it to his mouth. Eddie poked his nose out of Cole's jacket and licked the boy's chin.

Uncle Tran said to Lane, "I see now why you are good at what you do. We will find out if you are equally adept at keeping a secret."

Cole said, "The secret of what was inside the elephant? I'm really good at secrets."

"You might have to wait a while to learn this one." Rosie put her hand on the back of Cole's chair. She looked at Jay and winked.

"No I won't. It's obvious. The elephant was full of diamonds!" Cole said.

Everyone at the table looked at Uncle Tran. His face paled.

Rosie stared at Cole.

Cole shrank down into his chair, evading eye contact.

Tran noted Cole's reaction and smiled. "Jay tried to warn us about your intelligence. We should have listened. Cole?"

Cole continued to look away.

"You've just taught us all something," Uncle Tran said.

Cole looked at Uncle Tran. "Aren't adults supposed to teach kids?" Cole looked shocked at his own words and tone of voice he'd used to say it. He lifted another shrimp from the bowl. Eddie's head poked out of Cole's jacket. The dog snagged the shrimp from Cole's fingers.

Lane watched Cole, Jay, Uncle Tran, Harper, Tony, Loraine and Rosie. Their laughter spilled out. It was a crashing waterfall of emotions collected over weeks. Rosie put her palms on the table to brace herself so she wouldn't fall over. Tears rolled down Jay's cheeks. Eddie barked. It took Lane a moment to realize he was laughing with them.

more great mysteries from NeWest Press . . .

Queen's Park
A Detective Lane Mystery

GARRY RYAN

Detective Lane has a knack for discovering the whereabouts of missing persons. But the city's latest case has disappeared without a trace. After a brutal attack on his young nephew, ex-mayor Bob Swatsky has gone missing with 13 million dollars of tax-payers' money. Is he on the run with the cash, or is it something more sinister? A zany cast of characters, including a love doll, and a chain-smoking grandma with an oxygen tank, lead Detective Lane on a thrilling romp through the streets of Calgary. The chase is on, and alone, Lane must uncover the truth before someone ends up visiting Queen's Park cemetery . . . permanently.

ISBN 10: 1-896300-84-7 PB • ISBN 13: 978-1-896300-84-9
$10.95 CDN • $7.95 US

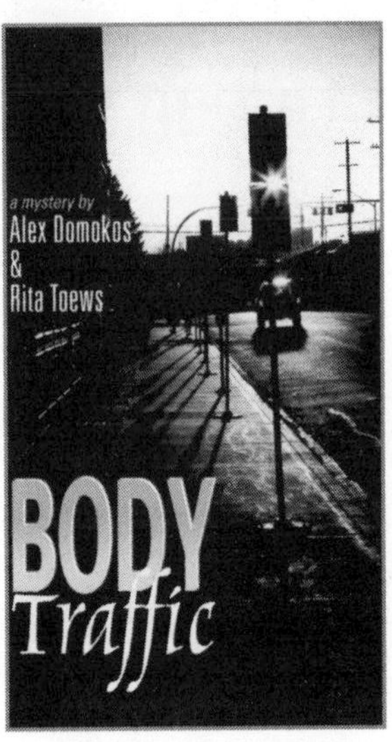

Body Traffic

ALEX DOMOKOS & RITA TOEWS

Relocated to Winnipeg, Undercover officer Stan Boyko soon finds himself working the meaner streets of the city, exposing a mess of lies and dirty dealings at a national forensic lab. Meanwhile, Sonja Sepsik is smuggled out of Ukraine into Hungary by her brother, and sold into a prostitution ring in Winnipeg. A chance meeting between Sonja and Stan gives the undercover officer a direct pipeline into the illegal activity, and gives Sonja the hope of escaping life on the streets. But when a brutal murder is committed, Sonja and Stan become tangled in a web of corruption that runs deeper than either of them ever imagined.

ISBN 10: 1-896300-96-0 PB • ISBN 13: 978-1-896300-96-2
$10.95 CDN • $7.95 US

A Deadly Little List

KAY STEWART & CHRIS BULLOCK

A deadly scandal surrounding a controversial land development casts a shadow over the annual Salt Spring Island theatre festival. While Constable Danutia Dranchuk searches desperately for clues surrounding an alleged suicide, nosey journalist Arthur Fairweather comes face to face with another mysterious death. Can they get to the bottom of all this madness before a third body is added to the list?

"*A Deadly Little List* is pure Gilbert and Sullivan . . . Chris and Kay take us backstage in this delicately crafted novel and show us the dirt—all the dirt.

—James Hawkins, *Crazy Lady*

ISBN 10: 1-896300-95-2 • ISBN 13: 978-1-896300-95-5
$11.95 CDN • $8.95 US

Acknowledgements

Bruce, for all things medical,
thank you.

For the toboggan idea,
thanks, Ben.

Kim, thanks for the
Oreo story.

Kent and Michael,
thanks for
the editing.

Ruth, Amber,
Rebecca, Katherine, Jennifer
and Doug
thanks for all that you do.

Thanks to creative writing students at
Nickle,
Bowness,
Lord Beaverbrook,
Alternative,
Forest Lawn and
Queen Elizabeth.

Sharon, Karma
and Luke,
thank you.

GARRY RYAN was born and lives in Calgary, Alberta, and has also lived in Singapore where he graduated from high school. Ryan received a B.Ed. and a Diploma in Educational Psychology from the University of Calgary, and teaches English and Creative Writing to junior high and high school students. He has been published in *The Globe and Mail Facts and Arguements*, *Alberta English*, *The ATA Magazine*, and *Alberta Poetry Yearbook*. Ryan has a passion for photography, and enjoys walking along the Bow River with his wife Sharon and their dog Scout. His first novel, *Queen's Park* (NeWest Press, 1-896300-84-7), sprung from a desire to write a mystery with an emphasis on the rich diversity and unique locations of his hometown. *The Lucky Elephant Restaurant* is the second title in his Detective Lane series.